Bristol Short Story Prize Anthology

Volume Fourteen

tangent
books

Bristol Short Story Prize Anthology Volume 14

First published 2021 by Tangent Books

Tangent Books, Unit 5.16 Paintworks
Bristol, BS4 3EH
0117 972 0645
www.tangentbooks.co.uk

Email: richard@tangentbooks.co.uk

ISBN: 9781914345128

Cover designed by Aitana Raguán-Hernández
www.aitanaraguan.com

Layout designed by Dave Oakley, Arnos Design
www.arnosdesign.co.uk

Printed and bound by
TJ Books, Padstow
Cornwall, PL28 8RW

A CIP catalogue record for this book is available from the British Library
www.tangentbooks.co.uk
www.bristolprize.co.uk

Contents

Introduction

The twenty stories shortlisted for the 2021 Bristol Short Story Prize and collected in this anthology, share a major feature: they create their own distinct atmospheres that demand to be read. They remained with our readers long after they were first encountered, and we hope they will have the same effect on you.

Many congratulations to the writers whose stories were shortlisted from 2,545 entries to this year's competition.

Third prize goes to Sarah Tinsley and her story, *I Don't Know What I've Lost*. Judge, Mahsuda Snaith says: "With brilliant imagery and cold realism amongst the surreal, *I Don't Know What I've Lost* reflects the sometimes exhausting, bewildering and conflicting feelings of first-time parenting. This story got my imagination firing and hit me in the gut with its vivid depiction of the rarely spoken about topic of the downside of parenting."

Sifters by Amanda Ong, her first short story publication, is awarded second prize. Judge Irene Baldoni says: "*Sifters* is literature in action – a touching, heartfelt act of memory and care, in this case even before someone we love has left us forever. The narrator knows that words cannot, ultimately, enclose a human existence in its wholeness and uniqueness. And yet they keep writing, gracefully, committing to paper one memory after the other, and we cannot but keep reading, thus becoming part of this attempt to defeat time."

This year's winning story is Isidora Cortes-Monroy's *Cake for the Disappeared*. Judge, Tom Robinson says the story has "an extraordinary mix of strangeness and poignancy and (is) an immensely difficult story to pull off. The balance of horror, humour, simplicity and humanity is beautifully handled."

We hope these three stories along with the other seventeen contained within these pages will provide you with unforgettable reading experiences.

The immense contributions of our readers and judges despite the continuing uncertainty around the pandemic have been crucial to the competition and the production of this anthology. A huge thank you to them.

Many thanks, also, to Mimi Thebo, Billy Kahora, Amy Lehain, Andi Bullard, Gruff Kennedy and Harry Boucher at Bristol University whose support and contributions have been so important to this year's activity.

The striking anthology cover is designed by recent University of the West of England Illustration degree graduate, Aitana Raguán-Hernández. Thanks to Aitana, to course leaders Chris Hill and Jonathan Ward and this year's 3rd year students for what continues to be an essential collaboration for us.

Biggest thanks go to the entrants to this year's competition for having the courage to share their words and their worlds, and for making it such an enlightening experience for us all. And, finally, to you for reading this collection. We hope you get as much from the stories as we have.

Joe Melia
BSSP Co-ordinator

1st Prize

Isidora Cortes-Monroy

Originally from Chile, but raised in Switzerland, Isidora has always navigated her intercultural world through literature. Having left her studies in Hotel Management in 2015, she went on to do a BA in English Literature and Spanish at the University of Manchester, an MPhil in Comparative Literatures at the University of Cambridge, and she will be starting a PhD in Hispanic Literatures at the University of Toronto this September. Earlier this year, she won her first writing competition, held by the Jane Austen Literary Foundation.

Cake for the Disappeared

It didn't surprise me the first night Joaquin didn't come back. He was always one to come home late. On most occasions he would return early the next morning, but there had been instances when we wouldn't see him for days. My mother, on the other hand, knew from the start that this time was different. We told her she was being dramatic, that she needn't worry, Joaquin was like that. She remained unconvinced.

At ten o'clock on that first morning, my mother baked a cake. This one was Joaquin's favourite, a milhojas de manjar. My mother had a special way of making it: the trick was to toast several handfuls of walnuts, crush them and spread them evenly between every layer, giving the cake an unexpected crunch. Once she had put on the final layer and had sprinkled a generous serving of crushed walnuts on top, she placed it on our dining table, washed her equipment and prepared her ingredients for the next recipe. She then baked a batch of chilenitos. Once those were done, she made a pot of arroz con leche. As soon as she finished it, she moved onto her well known brazo de reina. She spent her day walking back and forth between the kitchen and the dining table, placing on its surface each new pastry. By the time night had fallen and dinner time approached, the table seemed to have disappeared, submerged under a sea of desserts. My father and I, too scared to get in the way of my mother's cooking, decided it would be too complicated to cook a real meal, so we settled for a batch of cuchuflis for dinner. We ate by the window, watching the streets for any sign of Joaquin.

Breakfast the next day was no different, save for the assortment of desserts available to us. My mother had spent the whole night baking. With no more room left for desserts on the dining table, my mother had begun leaving them on the floor. The tide of food had now started creeping into the living room. By midday, the sofas were taken up by numerous trays and plates carefully balanced on their cushions. They look like they're in a meeting, my Dad joked. I laughed and suggested we eat the group leader for lunch. For the second time in twenty-four hours we filled up on dessert, this time cutting into a postre de tres leches that bled condensed milk.

By the second day, my father began to worry this was more than just a phase. We were quickly running out of habitable space as well as growing tired of these sweet meals. The first thing he did that morning was buy me a proper breakfast from the local market, making sure that my food was packed with the protein and vitamins I hadn't been able to eat the day before. He then began taking the trays of pastries to different neighbors' houses, begging them to accept as many as five or six desserts at a time. By lunchtime he had visited all our neighbors, yet the pile of deserts continued to grow, creeping into every crevice and hiding spot the house had to offer. Nothing was beyond their reach. Exasperated with the situation, my father loaded his car with as many delicacies as he could fit and drove to the market, in the hopes that he could sell them away. I stayed at home monitoring the street outside our house, in case Joaquin should return. By the time my father came back, the guest room and his own bedroom had been refilled with a new series of cakes.

A week had passed and nothing had changed, save for the number of rooms occupied by pastries. I was no longer surprised when I found an alfajor on my desk or a bag of hallullas stuffed inside my sock drawer. My room was no longer my own. Despite my father's efforts to sell the produce at the market, the tide continued to grow, spreading itself out across the house. He began to realize that as long as his wife continued to bake, we would never be rid of all the desserts, not even with the help of our family and neighbors.

He decided then to open a shop in the center of Santiago and sell her cakes there. It had never been my parents' ambition to open up their own shop, nor had my mother ever shown a particular interest in selling her pastries. But my father was out of options, and so he bought the first property he could find. He named my mother's bakery after her, *Dulce Soledad*. It took him a day to put up a few shelves and find a cash register. Besides those few basic elements, my father believed nothing else would be needed to sell my mother's desserts. His biggest concern wasn't the decorations or the marketing, but rather how to get my mother out of the house and into the shop. Throughout the course of three days we moved her utensils, making sure to only move a few at a time. On the last day we left a bowl and a whisk as the last pieces of equipment, planning to transfer my mother from the house to the shop while she whisked her egg whites into snowy peaks. By the time she reached her new workplace she had made a bowl of meringue and was demanding we give her back her piping tube. She made pajaritos dulces, piping the meringue into roses, each one with a missing petal.

My father, who could just about manage his taxes, now saw himself in the difficult situation of running a business. At first, our only customers were his family and friends who visited out of pure loyalty, or, as was more likely, a secret curiosity to see for themselves if the rumors about my mother were true. But before the first week had passed, we began to see new faces. Most were mothers like my own, although the ages ranged from the very young, who were expecting new children, to the elderly, who had seen their own grow up into parents themselves. With each payment they would nod and send their blessings to my mother in an unspoken pact of solidarity. I didn't understand these women but they understood my mother.

The queue to get inside grew longer with each passing day, stretching past our door and onto the street, sometimes even turning into the corner so that you couldn't see the end if you stood at the entrance. We were now attracting all types of customers, from all backgrounds and ages. For the first time on this street, the rich had to stand next to the poor and forgotten as each one waited their turn to be served. By the time the first month was up we had earned enough to redecorate our shop as well as hire additional help at the till, although my mother would never allow anyone else to work in her kitchen. She spent her nights and days baking, never leaving her post and only sleeping on her feet an hour a night. My father and I begged her to rest, but it had been weeks since she acknowledged anything we said to her. The only time she would momentarily stop was to ask if we'd heard anything about Joaquin. Each time we'd say no she'd return to her work with a renewed fervor.

We knew that sooner or later we would have to serve one of the uniformed. It was inevitable: we were a booming pastry shop set up a few blocks away from the offices at the Edificio Diego Portales, where they all worked. Everyone knew they had a sweet tooth, that they liked to indulge their appetite. Yet it still surprised us that day when we saw that green uniform step through our door and bolt it shut. He made his way across the room to the counter, ignoring the line of customers that had been left inside. Leaning over the counter with a smug smile, he examined the pastries behind me. I could smell a sour hint of garlic on his breath.

"When they told me this was the best bakery in all of Chile I didn't expect to find someone so young running it," he said after slowly licking his lips.

"It's not mine, sir," I answered. "My mother is the one who bakes. Can I get you anything?"

He pursed his lips, making his moustache and chin all the more prominent.

"Mija, it's sergeant, not sir. And yes," he said looking behind me, "I'll have a piece of that milhojas."

My father who had seen everything from the other side of the shop joined me behind the counter.

He cut the sergeant a generous portion of the cake, much larger than what he would normally give.

"It's what they're used to," he whispered. "That's why they're all guatones."

Without moving to let other customers past, the sergeant ate his cake over the counter, spilling crumbs onto the work surface on our side. When he finished, he wiped his mouth with a tissue my father gave him, leaving a trace of manjar on the corner of his moustache.

"I'm not sure what I expected," he said giving my father back the empty plate with the crumpled tissue, "but I can say I am surprised. Please send my regards to the chef, a truly remarkable woman. I can guarantee you'll be seeing a lot more of us now."

Without so much as a goodbye, he turned and strolled out, parting the line of customers that had watched everything in a sober silence. Before serving the next customer, my father made me swear I wouldn't tell my mother what had happened. I told him I wouldn't, knowing well that my mother always kept the kitchen door open anyway.

Despite the sergeant's promise, we didn't see another uniform in the shop until a couple of weeks after the first visit. Unlike the sergeant, the officer that came this time waited his turn in the line, listening nervously to the woman beside him who had a list of complaints regarding a security guard on her block. When he arrived at the counter, I noticed that instead of medals, his jacket was adorned with two sweat patches.

"I've come with an order from the offices at the Edificio Diego Portales requesting that the present bakery cease its deliveries of baked goods immediately we are thankful for the products you have continuously sent to us nonetheless as of today your services are no longer required nor welcomed," he said in one breath. I could tell from the way he squinted his eyes that he had been told to memorize and repeat the order word for word.

With a large grin on his face, my father reached for a berlin on the shelf behind him, wrapped it in a napkin and put it on the counter in front of the officer.

"Whilst my daughter and I would gladly respect such a request," he answered, "I must clarify that we haven't sent any cakes to the Edificio Diego Portales. And please," he gestured at the berlin on the counter, "help yourself to one of our specialties. On the house."

It took a few seconds for the officer to react. Confused, he picked up the berlin, looking from my father to the cake and back again. I noticed his upper lip had a thin moustache, no thicker than the one

Joaquin had tried to grow before he disappeared.

"But you d-do," he finally stuttered. "Every day we receive hundreds of your cakes."

My father shook his head and shrugged his shoulders.

"Wherever you're getting them from, I can promise you they're not from here."

The young officer's eyebrows furrowed as he searched for a response. Unable to find the right words, he turned and left. We could see him through the shop window as he unwrapped the berlin and nibbled it, his face still distorted by the scowl that hadn't left. He didn't notice the bit of custard that fell onto his uniform.

Every day after that visit we would attend one of the uniformed. They each came with the same request, leaving with the same answer and a pastry which they invariably ate before they were out of sight. It became common knowledge that the men at the Edificio Diego Portales were struggling to contain the large volumes of cake they received every day. People described the way these desserts appeared in their filing cabinets or in their drawers, how it wasn't uncommon for an official to accidently sit on an empolvado and to be seen walking around with powdered sugar on his bottom. There had even been a rumor that because of a jam stain on a document, a police unit not too far from us had received an order of five hundred balloons instead of batons.

It wasn't long after this final incident that we saw a large military van pull up to the shop. Sensing something had changed, my mother emerged from the kitchen with a bowl in her arms. She was mixing the dough for a dozen tacitas. Through the shop window, the three of us watched as the military men opened the door and threw out one cake after another onto the street, as if they were bags of coal rather than carefully assembled pastries. Once they had emptied their cargo, they jumped back in the van and drove off, leaving the thick carpet of smashed desserts on the pavement that was already attracting nearby flies.

For the first time since Joaquin's disappearance, I saw my mother put down the mixing bowl. Without saying a word, she stormed out of the shop. My father and I followed closely behind, ordering one of the apprentices to watch the till while we were gone. There was no need for that though, as the line of customers that had been snaking into our shop soon followed my mother. At the pace she walked, it didn't take long for us to arrive at the Edificio Diego Portales, its glass structure looming over the crowd as we stood outside its main entrance. On the lawn in front of the building sat an assortment of pastries. The collection grew by the minute as officials coming in and out of the building deposited new desserts on the grass. Through the glass doors we could see the receptionist hiding behind the rows of cakes that had piled up on the desk's surface.

My mother picked up the nearest pastry, a pie de limón, and carried it into the reception, quickly leaving before the receptionist could say anything. She repeated the act, bringing back into the building the cakes the officials had left on the lawn, ignoring the receptionist's protests each time she entered the building. Bewildered, many of the officials who had been carrying cakes outside stood still, marveled by my mother's determination as she carried up to ten cakes at a time. None of them dared intervene, knowing well not to get in the way of a mother's anger. Finally, the youngest of the officers approached her. His uniform was cleaner and smoother than the others, perhaps being used for the first time. As my mother bent down to pick up a raspberry meringue cake, the officer tapped her on the shoulder, touching her so lightly that it took her a while to realize he was there.

"Señora," he said quietly, "what are you doing? Why don't you go home? This is no place for a woman like you."

My mother tightened her grip on the cake, her fingers digging into the pink meringue.

"I'll go when you tell me where my son is," she snarled.

"I'm sorry, I don't know who –"

"Joaquin," she spat. "Where is he?"

She threw the cake into his hands, covering his thin fingers in its pink sludge. Turning to a nearby officer she asked him the same question. He didn't answer. She looked for another officer, and then another, her voice growing louder each time she repeated the question.

"Where is he?" she cried.

Forty-five years later we're still asking the same question.

2nd Prize
Amanda Ong

Amanda Ong (she/her) is a writer from California currently based in Seattle, USA. She graduated from Columbia University in 2020 cum laude with degrees in Creative Writing and Ethnicity and Race Studies. There, Amanda was the recipient of Departmental Honors and the Center for Ethnicity and Race Studies' Award for Academic Excellence. Concepts of oral history, material culture, subjectivity, and radical justice are consistent influences in her writing. College campus literary magazines aside, *Sifters* is her first published short story, and she could not be more delighted.

Sifters

We get away with it by being earnest.

Who struck first, you or I? I know I said I want to live a million different lives. I said I want to live the life of everyone I know. I want to live yours. I want to live mine but different, and then again, and again, and again, and again.

And you said: It's possible.

This is my favorite story because nothing bad happens in it. Some time ago I asked you how we came here from being so small; your knuckles, wrinkled, and cheeks, sallow. I liked to pinch and stretch the thin, loosened skin of your hands, take close looks at your finger bones, long and brittle, where your veins, bright green, sat against the surface.

You said, Came where from being small? You noted that I at least had not gone anywhere, still small really, and I asked you if you remembered taking me to my first grade parent teacher conference. Did you see how small the elementary school toilets were? Miniscule. The tiniest toilets made for the tiniest little butts.

But I was so tiny too. That year I wanted a milk frother so badly I put it at the top of my Christmas list. Someone, maybe my mother, maybe you, let me taste a sip of their latte and I could not stop thinking about the white puffs of foam overflowing the cup for months after. How was such a thing possible! How could I make it possible? I'm unsure who told me what a frother was, or even if anyone had really told me, but I asked doggedly for my own cloud-milk. I wasn't given one that Christmas and I cried boldly, buried beneath my much more suitable presents. My parents wrote it off as my being still small and spoiled, and they were right. But you picked me up from school a few weeks later, took me to the nearest megamall and let me choose the cheapest milk frother. It was a small battery powered stick with a coiled whisk that spun at the touch of a button. We went home and made the fluffiest hot chocolate I had ever had with it, and I was content because you indulged me, because you were the only one to indulge me. And for you to do so was to indulge yourself, to allow both of us some kind of frivolity, to share a small secret delight that no one else could see.

But I asked and you didn't remember any of this. Was I sure it wasn't my mother who had gone with me to the parent teacher conference? Or my father who had given me the frother? It seemed like something he would do. From the moment I was born you said that he had a hard time not giving me what I asked for if he had the means for it. You said you told him that it wasn't good to spoil children, that you needed to show them a bit of tough love. But you also understood; you said it was hard not to be the same way with him when he was a child.

I wanted to scream. I wanted to slap you across the knuckles the way you used to when I would play "Chopsticks" on the piano instead of "Für Elise." How could you forget so cavalierly? The tiny toilets or the milk frother, these things had been so hilarious, so important once. You said go ahead, scream. It is the first sound we know how to make, why stop there? The things you remembered were still different from the things I did.

Instead, you remembered when you used to bathe me, how you gently dipped my head into the warm water, how my eyes would close and how small I was and how you, sometime back before all of this, had some role in creating me. And I would emerge from the water with my hair dripping wet, slicked back, and ask you if I looked like Gōng Gōng now with my hair like this. You remembered how I liked to press the mole on your forehead and say, "Ding dong! Is the door open?" You remembered that I liked soup so much I would take the straw from my juice in restaurants and slurp down the broth. It always used to make you laugh.

I couldn't remember this. I wanted to ask how we could remember so differently but you just shrugged. You said it was okay, something about how every person's memories are their own reality, just dreams or alternate lives, and the more things you dream, the more likely one of them is to be real.

Maybe I had forgotten too. But I love you and I talk too much, so that was that.

In the time between then and when I see you next, everything is normal. I go to classes. I wear my headphones and listen to music by myself. I walk along sidewalks and up stairs and down streets. My mother is the one who calls me to share status updates on you. Everything is normal even when she tells me how you have gotten worse.

At school I use the bathroom stall next to the window every time. The window is frosted and three floors up so no one can see you, but you can still peer outside. In my experience it has always been left open, just a crack, and in the winter it lets in a tight chill that I feel while I pee. I never close it; I look and watch the people pass by. They go in their hoards, colors, in splotches and murders and cohorts and

21

dapples of paint. I think about how many of these people I know and how many I have never encountered before and how many I have met or crossed paths with countless times before and don't even know it. I think about the likelihood of each, and isn't it kind of a miraculous thing? I use that bathroom stall for months before one day I catch a faint whiff of leftover smoke and realize why someone has been leaving the window open all of this time.

You call me once, by accident. You were trying to call my father. But you don't stutter when you realize you have reached me instead – you apologize profusely. You say you're so sorry; you forgot the recipe for the almond cookies you used to bake for me. I forgot about them, or that I had even asked you for the recipe. Why did you remember this of all things? This slice of our lives that has intersected, and it is not a thing I remember. I say I forgive you, but you don't stop saying sorry. I ask if that's all you called about. You say you meant to call my father, and I say Ok, I love you, and we hang up.

I choose to think about you even when I don't have to. I could be thinking of anything else. You're escapable. But I want to make myself think of you. I want to remember every ounce of you I can, every detail of every moment that we have lived in together before. I want to memorize you so well that I know exactly who you were in your lifetime before me and your days now without me. Is that what processing is? I'm not sure. I've never processed.

When I take the night bus to see you two states up, I sit next to a man I have no intention of talking to. I don't usually talk to strangers. You taught me that. I thought I would use that time to remember you better, but then he asked, Where are you headed?

And it all slipped out from under me.

I did not talk about you really, but I found every way I could to talk around you – a gaping negative space in my speech. I talked about me and him and her and, and, and you were there in all of it. More of myself could be revealed in two hours than I had ever known before, not when I have spent several lifetimes just trying to un-reveal myself to you. After the bus ride was over, we exchanged nothing. I left and felt homesick for him, a stranger I missed immediately, like family.

I wake up with gunk in my eyes that I can't blink out and I go to visit you. By the time I arrive, the world is still blurry and solid. I have never visited the home you are in now, but despite the spots in my vision I can see that the walls are mint green. I can think only of when I went to Chicago last spring and visited the Public Housing Museum – all of the major museums were farther from my hotel, and admission was free. Testimonies from the now-elderly who grew up in public housing sixty, seventy years ago, all recounted the bright mint green walls across each complex in the city. They later found that the paint was full of lead, was responsible for poisoning dozens of its tenants, children and old and all poor. But the now-elderly remember that shade of mint-green, the walls with nostalgia, fond dinner table memories that they have left behind. A generation of folks raised in our nation's poor attempt at offering necessity, now torn up and googly-eyed about lead. I will myself not to worry if there is lead in your walls.

Your room is simple. I take inventory. Pastel set of hand towels. Mop and bucket. Stick with a claw at the end, made to grab things far away. Same calligraphy on the walls above your small twin bed as you have always had.

Your caretaker's name is Mary, and she takes me to your room where you are setting up chess. I still cannot see well, but you are uneasy on your legs now. You see me. It has been months since we have seen each other and you say, Oh, you. Come play with me. I have been wondering when you would turn up.

You do not beat me easily as you used to, but you do beat me. You laugh in your victory and shake your head. You point at the calligraphy on the walls, and you say, You see this? You know I wrote these myself?

I nod, because this is a fact of my life as much as it is of yours. I know, I tell you. They're very beautiful.

It's impressive, isn't it? Can you write poetry? Can you do calligraphy? I smile. No, I can't. But my handwriting is excellent.

Then you take after me! You say, and that makes me laugh too.

You ask me if I'm seeing anyone. I am not and have not been, and I say so.

You shake your head. Then they are missing out. Find someone who writes poetry, why don't you? Marry someone who makes beautiful calligraphy like me!

I giggle more, because god, who needs to date more poets.

So then, you say. Anything else happening in your life?

I was in a car accident last week; I tell you even though I have no right to say it.

Are you okay?

I am eager to nod, to assure you yes. It's funny, how I'm more and more accustomed to not being able to explain these things to you. I say, I'm fine. No one was hurt. I say that the car was old anyways.

I want to say that it was my fault, absolutely nothing to blame but my incompetence. I do not retell the feeling of spiraling, of no control, of being sent off, off the road, over the sidewalk, into the dirt. Of coming out the other end, unsure what worlds I had passed through. Of the firm possibility of no worlds at all. I do not tell you how I hate driving; something you had once known about me that I am sure you cannot remember now. I could tell you all of these things but the likelihood is that you will remember none of them. I could confide this in you but it would be a blip, a glitch, a fork in our realities.

You ask me again if I am okay, and I smile and nod with force. You relax. You will forget.

Mary sits in the corner. She eats half a raw onion between two slices of bread and tells me she has lost thirty pounds this way. I make a face and sputter, and you laugh.

Mary says that my face is too gaunt. You shake your head harshly. You have a good face. A lucky face, you say.

I have a face like yours, I want to say, I always have. But I thank you and nod, and that is enough for now.

By then, I build up the courage to ask you if you remember my name. I do not flinch when you say that you do not. You close your eyes and hold your temples, and again say No, no I do not. But I know who you are, you say without pretense. I know you.

You become too tired to talk, so we sort through a box of old photos. They are fuzzy, from quality or my eyesight, I can't tell. Each holds its own memory, its own version of you. Ones in high fashion, at the beach, drinks in hand. Or disheveled. Unhappy looking. With friends. Ones of the two of us. Photos of wartime, peacetime, of you at near half and near twice your current weight. You are quiet save for when I find a photo of an old lover, dated and signed. I say ooh, who is this? One of many? You cluck and tell me that's not fair. It was a different lifetime.

I want you to talk more. I want you to be vigorous, to remember, to tell me everything before me in photos, now only photos and nothing else. I am not satiated – it never feels like enough for us to just sift through these memories and no more, parts without whole. We are still living in separate realities, even the pieces we do share left disparate. I ask Mary if you have been eating well, sleeping well, exercising enough. You speak up then, and say yes, I do. But you refuse to take walks with Mary and she won't let you walk on your own.

But I'm fine, you say. I'm well. I do not need anything.

I ask you if you will walk with me, and you look at me, eyes wide, and say, Of course I'll walk with you. I love you!

I think that maybe if I am quiet enough, really, really quiet, all of my want will stop. And if my want stops, I might have room for other things, room to handle the brazenness of this moment. I have the compulsion to ask you again if you remember my name, if you remember the tiny toilets or the milk frother, or if I told you about my life now would you be able to remember. I wonder how much of your memory is yours, how much it is of something else entirely.

Mary puts you down for a nap, while I make a cutting from your jade plant to take home. You taught me how to make cuttings years ago, and I have never forgotten. The first cutting I took home from your house I planted in the backyard and let sit in the sun until it withered, until its thick, plump leaves shriveled and fell, until its skin became too tough to puncture with the tip of my thumbnail the way healthy jades do, translucent and jelly-like. I had named her Janet.

When she died, I covered her remains with dirt and held a ceremony. The issue with cuttings was always just that; one living jade could either die or be salvaged through a snip and the replanting of roots. A branch masquerades as a whole. It splits and they, of the same stem, arch into new, alternate beings made of identical matter, no longer knowing the life of their own other, now being lived without them. Janet in the end was some same bit of your jade that I took and let live another life, as is the jade I take now. I take paper towels, wrap the jade inside and tuck my cutting into a used grocery bag.

You seem so much smaller when you sleep. This is the first time I have seen you where I have heard you breathe in every moment, a quiet confirmation of the force of your life. The last time I saw you we talked about what was difficult about coming to America, and you said the language. You said English is so confusing. Wiener? Hot dog? Wiener? Which was it? And I laughed and laughed and laughed and you did not understand what I thought was so funny.

Our best moments are always when I have lived through you. And you have allowed me to, and I have had so many questions – who else were you? Have I met all of you? Were you hungry? What for? You told me it had once been a luxury to eat ketchup with your rice instead of dirt, never enough to fill you up, that you once ran to freedom, that bombs fell across your childhood. I read once that it took seven generations after the Irish famine for Irish women to become fully healthy again. I am two generations from you, so what does that make me? Maybe my body is not at full capacity. Maybe I am a step in the process of recharging. Maybe I am lacking, not the fullest incarnation, but I would never want to be even a step further away from you, not willingly, no matter what I myself might lose. I will not lose the part of me that is you.

In childhood, Dad told me that humans never truly touch anything. There is always the smallest sliver of space between us, separating us from everything else, what we feel just the impression of the surface. I was so angry with him, frustrated with the knowledge that I would never touch anything in my life, never really feel anything but my own distance from all else. But I know better now what the answers are. If everything were right, I would have no distance at all from you or the world or the other people who pass by, until we fuse and meld like burning metal. But this is not feasible now. I must be content at least to not be of a later generation, a final step, where you are an echo and I am a whole. I am content to be partial with you.

This is my favorite story because nothing bad happens in it.

We retreat here. We live: in your home with the vines, or your old home with the garden, or the childhood home I have never seen. You paint calligraphy on Mondays or Sundays or Fridays and it is sun and winter and spring and snow and the world is beautiful. We make mountains of froth atop hot chocolate wonders and laugh about tiny toilets and know every person who passes by on the street. Accidents do not exist. You do not have to choose between hot dog and wiener, the walls are mint green and free of lead, jade plants grow in excess and we never forget. Music plays all of the time and everyone can hear it. I meet every one of you in your photos. There is no distance between us, and you are me and I am you and all our memories are whole. We scream when we want to. The door is always open.

3rd Prize
Sarah Tinsley

Sarah Tinsley is a UK writer living in France who writes fiction and non-fiction. She's drawn to exploring gender issues and helping others explore their creative selves. Her first novel won the Spread the Word/Bookouture competition in 2020 and is due to be released in January 2022. Her short fiction has been published widely, including in *Mslexia* and *Litro* and she has an MA in Creative Writing from City University. She runs workshops and coordinates Write By You, a community writing project for underrepresented young female writers in the UK. For more visit https://sarahtinsley.com and follow @ sarahtinsleyuk

I Don't Know
What I've Lost

On Wednesday morning there was a mouse in the bathtub. Ali could hear it scrabbling while she tried to solve the snot problem. The yellow sucker thing that looked like a tiny turkey baster didn't work. If Becka couldn't breathe she couldn't eat, and if she couldn't eat she wouldn't sleep.

Peering over the edge of the bath, she saw a small white body. It looked up at her, twitching. Pink eyes and worm tail. The baby had sat there last night, a crease in her lips that could have been a smile as Ali squirted her with the plastic whale. As she watched, the mouse shuddered and deposited a poo next to the yellow sponge. She reared back, a wail of disgust in the back of her throat.

Becka lay on the mat, the obstruction in her nose increasing her usual pig-snuffle. Ali opened the bathroom cabinet, intent on a solution. Jars, bottles and tubes overflowed from the baskets she'd bought to try and keep everything organised. This one for colic, that one for an allergic reaction, three types of thermometer. Each morning she gave a list to Lorna after reading another article about baby illnesses.

The tweezers. Of course. That would work. She grappled Becka into the crook of one arm. Turning the fluorescent light on, she peered up the tiny nose. Her first attempt pushed the big lump of snot in further. The second grazed the edges and slipped off. She sighed, shuffled, a prickle of pain starting in her neck.

This time she would not be defeated. She roamed around in there, going further in so she could grip it, finally pulling it out with a faint sucking noise.

The sound of scratching claws and she froze, horrified. What if Becka had moved her head? One baby-doll loll in the wrong direction and the tweezers would go right up. Stick in her soft, barely-formed brain. Blood would trickle down as the tiny body cooled and stiffened. It repeated – a vivid short film, draining a hollow in her stomach.

'You got the mega bogey.' Lorna walked in and picked up her hairbrush. 'Are you going to that baby group again today?' She leaned over and squeezed a fat leg.

'Might do.'

So far her pretend outings had included Sensory Immersion, Baby Pilates and Massage Mindfulness. She hadn't left the house in six weeks.

'Good for you.' Lorna turned around, reached into the bath.

'No!' Ali clattered the tweezers into the sink.

'What's wrong?' She turned, sponge in one hand. Couldn't she see it?

'Just, you know. Here we go again.' Ali put Becka down and lifted up her legs to reveal the yellow-stained bottom.

'Sorry, love. I'm clocking out.' Lorna kissed them both and left. Such a simple action. Opening a door and going through it.

She wrangled Becka's limbs into a babygro. Swept the brush over her head, avoiding the soft bit. What if she slipped and gave her brain damage? She'd read an article at four in the morning about a baby that managed to hang itself on the strings of a window blind.

The mouse started scrabbling again. Ali shuddered, picked Becka up and closed the door. Her quick exit meant she hadn't been able to check the snot. She'd wanted to take a picture, check if it was the right colour.

In the first few weeks she'd photographed everything. The poo in the nappies looked like the luminous curry sauce you got from the chip shop. That couldn't be right. Her entire nipple wasn't in the baby's mouth – did that mean the latch was wrong? The nappies kept leaking – was she doing them up properly? All that research into cloth nappies and now she was fumbling around with poppers while worrying the baby was getting cold. A red-prickle rash sat like a belt around her tummy, despite using the organic vegan cream she'd found online.

Then there were the night videos. This half-moaning wail that sounded like crying, but in the light from the white noise machine Becka's eyes were closed. Surely she wasn't sleeping. Was she in pain? Was this normal? She sent them to her sister, her mum, anyone she'd met who had kids. Was this right? Was any of it right?

The responses varied. Some didn't remember. Said it had been too long ago. Ali couldn't fathom how anyone could forget this intense fever dream. Others replied with laughing smileys. Welcome to the club. Oh I remember that. Lol what a nightmare. Haha now you understand.

So everyone else had been fine. Had known what to do. She didn't send anymore videos. With the baby asleep on her knees she scrolled through the photos she'd taken of red marks on the velvet skin and compared them to online images of hives and ringworm, reading but not commenting on forums to see traces of herself in other people's despair.

And now she had to call someone. Engage in conversation so they could come and deal with the mouse problem. She imagined the shapes the words would make as they left her mouth. Practised 'hello' in front of the mirror until it didn't sound like a distress call.

She put Becka down on the bed and sat next to her. Exhaustion was like an illness. It crept up her spine, pulled her down onto the bed. Maybe they could lie there, the two of them. Get her strength up before calling. She shuffled the baby further away and put her head down. Sleep sat over her, waiting.

The death rate from SIDS was increased when the baby slept in the parental bed. Then there was the possibility that she would learn to roll over, crash to the floor and break her skull on the laminate flooring they put in last year.

She forced herself up. Coffee and food would help. Decaf of course, but it might fool her body into waking. Getting dressed would create the illusion of having somewhere to go.

She opened her wardrobe and found a sloth hanging on the rail. Its bandit eyes watched her, one paw reaching at shutter-click speed to reach the cuff of her favourite shirt and place it in its mouth.

They would take the baby away. Seeing things that weren't there. She was unfit. As if in agreement, Becka made a grumbling sound from the bed. A shiver of delight. She could sleep. For as long as she wanted. Sit and eat steak and mushrooms, really taste them instead of cramming stuff in her mouth while the baby fed so she didn't get the shakes. See her friends, go to the Sylvan Post and drink yellow ale with a packet of unfurled crisps in the middle of the table.

As she assembled a collage of all the things she'd lost, a tortoise walked into the room. A wash of self-loathing as she realised she'd wished her baby into non-existence. The creature took a ponderous step on the faux mahogany floor. Black eyes glared up at her, head waving in condemnation.

It was time to get out of the house.

On the bus, a woman stared. She was rocking a pram vigorously with one hand. Wearing one of those kaftan things that looked stylish on other people but made Ali look like a misshapen tent. She touched her face. Maybe she had sick in her hair, milk on her coat.

It had taken almost an hour to get out of the house. A top-up feed, fifteen minutes of wrestling with the sling that was nothing but a very big scarf before putting the fluffy all-in-one on Becka and placing her in the pram. Then she'd done a poo, so another change of everything including the coat that had somehow got stained.

Then herself. Coat and shoes and a hat to hide her unwashed hair. She'd leant against the front door, remembered how she waddled to work just a few months ago. That was around the time she went to carnival. All her younger friends thought she was cool for still going even though she was seven months pregnant. How she held her hands over the bump, told the squiggle of life inside that they should get used to this throbbing noise. They talked about going to a festival with her in the summer. As if that would happen now. Then the tortoise had appeared in the hall and she'd rushed out before she could see any more animals.

'I see you've got one too.' The woman rattled the snakeskin bag in her hand, pointed at the carrier underneath Ali's pushchair.

'What?' She looked down. Nestled between the change bag, spare nappies and emergency pork scratchings, she could see a shell. There was a scrunching sound as it rubbed one leg against the packet.

'Grief tortoise.' The woman opened her bag. There were two small tortoises huddled next to her wallet. She'd lined the bag with straw.

'You have two.' Ali couldn't think of anything else to say.

'Miscarriages. Took us a while to get this one.' She pushed back the hood of her pram. Inside it, a pink face peered out between layers of cloth. It didn't look much bigger than Becka. The pram was one of those fancy ones with three wheels.

'I'm sorry.' She hadn't dared to say that word out loud. It had happened to someone at work. Months later they'd mumbled something about losing it, as if it were a misplaced sock.

'You've got a big one.' She was talking so loud. 'Did someone in your family die? A grandparent?'

'No.' Her granddad died when she was eighteen. After that, nothing but good health for everyone she cared about. It made her worry she wouldn't be a resilient parent.

'Want to get coffee?' The woman tucked the bag over her shoulder. She was even wearing earrings.

'I don't want it.' She pictured the swinging thing in her wardrobe, the twitching nose in her bathtub.

'I took them all the way to Ealing once and left them there.' She clicked something and the pram handle slid out. 'They made it back to the house before dark. Thought they'd disappear once he turned up.' She nodded at the baby. Its tongue was sticking out. 'You coming?'

'I need to get a mousetrap.' She wasn't going to waste her first morning out of the house with someone who had washed and was wearing make-up.

'Don't feed it cucumber, you'll never get the stains out.' She smiled and levered the pram off the bus. Becka started fussing. The rustling sound increased. It had got into the pork scratchings.

She found the nearest Argos and flicked through the catalogue, ignoring the sound of crunching. Becka wailed and she found she could be that woman – the one who let the grating sound of their child annoy everyone else because it had become background noise.

She put the kettle on when they got home. Walked into the bathroom, put the mousetrap in the bath and then put the plug in and turned the taps on. Filling the largest pot they had with boiling water, she scooped up the shell with its waggling feet and shoved it in the pot, turning the heat on underneath. She took thick electric tape and sealed all of the gaps around the wardrobe door.

The sound of rushing, bubbling water accompanied her back to the bedroom as she put Becka down onto the bed and collapsed next to her. Sleep came and sat on her until the next feed.

She disposed of the bodies in the garden after mopping the floor. Put rubber gloves on and shoved them all in a bin bag. Digging into the earth was far more satisfying than the Mindfulness app she'd downloaded. That droning voice was just an annoyance as she searched for solutions to Becka's lack of sleep – never more than three hours in a row.

She heard the door while she was rinsing mud off the gloves.

'Where's my girl?' Lorna came into the kitchen using that strange voice that had arrived with the baby.

'Don't, she's asleep.'

The baby bouncer was perched on the kitchen table. She couldn't lie in it for too long, it would curl her spine.

'You two had a good day?' Lorna stayed too close, touching Becka's feet.

'The usual.'

All those hours with nothing in them. Topping up the water bottles around the house, making three sandwiches and piling biscuits and bananas on the plate in the few minutes Becka would stay asleep in the moses basket, lying down on the bed for a stolen thirty minutes, furious that the scrambled panic in her head wouldn't let her sleep.

'Must be nice with her sleeping so much.' Lorna flopped down at the kitchen table. 'This deal is dragging on.'

'Is that why you're late?' No more post-six o'clock texts after the argument last week. The time moved so slowly.

'Please. I was one of the first to leave.' She got her phone out. Clearly bored with them already.

'They know you've got a small baby,' Ali said.

They'd talked about applying for Shared Parental Leave, then realised they couldn't afford it, not on Ali's teacher wages.

'Unless I popped it out, they don't want to know.' Lorna smiled, stretched her arms above her head. 'The guy took us outside to do circuits in the sun today. Managed my first set of burpees without stopping. My triceps are killing me.'

Everything about her was so normal.

'I can't imagine.' Ali turned back to the sink and shook water off the gloves. She remembered the bodies in the ground.

'You'll be done with mat leave soon. Only seven months left, you big slacker.' Lorna was up again, rummaging in the cupboards.

'Right.' It was a joke, of course it was a joke. No need to snap.

Every day Ali kept checking her phone to check what day it was. The boundaries between them had dissolved. But she still had a sense of time, the enormous desert of it lying before her. Seven whole months. Alone.

'You're doing so well.' Lorna came over and put her head on Ali's shoulder, took her hand. She must have noticed. It must be obvious.

'I'm not.' At the touch on her skin, she felt the edge of her blanket of competence start to unravel. 'Maybe you could stay home tomorrow?'

'I wish. We've got the Malaysians coming in for that meeting. And you know what that means.'

'Quaffing with Clients.' Ali used to go along to those, pretend to be a business associate and wear fake glasses. Lorna wouldn't be home until gone midnight.

Becka squawked awake. Lorna turned. 'Oh, honey.' She scooped her up.

'Tell them you've got a baby. That I need help.' How gently she held Becka. That look on her face.

'Come on, don't ask me that.' Lorna didn't look up.

'It's the same for you, isn't it? Nothing's changed. Not a bloody thing.' Ali threw the gloves in the sink.

'Go and lie down or something. I'll make dinner. You're always grumpy when you're tired.' Lorna turned away, cradling the little thing.

Yes, she helped. Washing, cooking, cleaning, organising the birth certificate. These tiny efforts drained away so quickly. Her identity hadn't shifted. Ali was a feeding station, a pillow, an inanimate object pouring love over something that didn't respond. She was a changeling.

In the weeks before the birth when Ali was too big to sleep they stayed up late making promises to each other. Having seen the disintegration of her sister's social life and career, she kept checking – we won't be like that, will we? That won't be us. Lorna had stroked her hair, her bump, told her they were going to do it together.

By the end of the week there were three dead mice, each one glaring white against the ground before she covered it over. She even managed to open the lid when she boiled the second tortoise. It stank the house out and she had to have two showers afterwards, one foot on the baby bouncer as she rinsed the stench out of her hair.

The third one wouldn't come out from under the cot. It lurked there as if it knew her intentions – perhaps it could smell the taint of tortoise flesh in the air. So much for taking matters into her own hands.

*

A week later she found the woman on the same bus. This time her twin tortoises were swinging from the pram in a net bag. She was wearing a cashmere shawl and her nails were painted. Ali barged down the aisle with the pram to where the woman was standing, swiping her phone in the disabled space.

'They won't go away,' Ali said. She didn't bother checking the pram anymore. Somehow it was always there.

'There's a wine bar round the corner that has a creche.' She lowered her phone and smiled. 'I'm Olive.'

They put their babies on the floor. There were soft lights and music. On the ceiling, a disco ball. The waiter brought over a menu, a bowl of seasoned chickpeas and a sample of their latest Bordeaux.

'So. What's happening?' Olive put a socked foot on her baby's tummy. 'She hates not having contact with me.'

Ali nodded, as if she also had an instinct for what her baby wanted.

'There's a mouse. Well, several. I drowned the first one. The others got caught in the trap. And I boiled two tortoises. It didn't work. There's another one hiding under the cot.' Ali dangled plastic keys over Becka's head. The baby's eyes crossed, a jerk of limbs as she squeaked with excitement.

'I like your style.' Olive waved the waiter over. 'One Cab Sav, one Bordeaux.' She barely looked at him.

'You don't have any others?' Ali pulled at her maternity top with the flowers on. There was a white stain on the left boob. She was running out of clothes. Lorna had asked about the tape on the wardrobe but she couldn't bring herself to take it off. Somehow that body would be worse.

'Just these three.' She gestured to the bag. One of them was eating a lettuce leaf.

'My flat is small. And my partner thinks I'm crazy.' The waiter arrived and placed the glasses down with patterned coasters underneath. Ali grabbed one of them before he left. 'Well, more than before.'

'Men just don't understand.' Olive swapped her feet over. She was wearing odd socks.

'She's a woman. I thought it would make a difference. Women are supposed to be more empathetic.' But the differences still gaped. Lorna's body wasn't stretched out, her hormones erratic. She was so calm in the face of Becka's needs.

'Oh.' Olive leaned back, picked up the other glass. 'How did you manage that?' The same question. As if it would be fine for her to ask what position proved successful for straight couples.

'Do other people have them?' Ali was feeling giddy. She hadn't drunk anything since the birth.

'I saw a man with a ferret on a lead once. It might have been a pet.' Olive shrugged. She didn't seem bothered by her strange reptiles.

'I need to get rid of them.' It was bad enough dealing with one new body in the house.

'Ok.' Olive swept the baby up with one hand, glass still in the other. 'Try noticing.'

'I don't think that's a problem. They're everywhere.'

'How you feel. Just before they move, or you see them.' She put her glass down, leaned over and gave the other one a leaf. 'Sometimes I don't see them for a while. Then I think about it and there they are.' She shook her head. 'We planted one flower for each – a lavender and a monkshood – to remember them by. When we came back from holiday next door's cat had dug them up and done a massive crap in the planter.' Her voice was quiet now. 'After the first one I didn't stop bleeding for six weeks. I got the second one taken out under anaesthetic.' Olive swayed, bracelets jangling.

'I'm sorry.' She'd forgotten that other people could wear the disguise of capability. They finished their drinks and let the tortoises have a race on the play mat. On the way home she bought a lettuce.

That night was one of the worst. The longest Becka stayed in noisy sleep was two hours. Each time Ali lurched upright her head was thick. She sat in the chair in the living room, cramming cereal bars and water into her mouth for forty minutes while the tiny chin pulsed against her skin.

At three she picked up her phone. It was open on the last article she'd been reading – apparently the tortoise was a symbol of endurance, of wealth. So why was it here? Olive said it was for grief. But someone had arrived in her life, not left.

Becka snuffled, her head falling away. Mouth open, eyes half-closed and glassy. Such satisfaction. Ali touched the tulip mouth, imagined all the ways she could ruin this beautiful thing. Tight coils of possibility wound into each cell of her.

They had to start going to classes. She was going to end up stunted. On the app there was a Tooting Tots music class at 10am. That meant getting out of the house by nine at the latest. Getting dressed. Preparing the bag. She slumped further down in the chair.

A scraping sound. The sloth hung from the curtain rail, claws tapping at the window. If anything she felt relieved. At least there wasn't a furry body stiffening in her wardrobe. She saw her own lethargy in its subdued speed. Maybe they could stay at home.

On the fifth feed the sky was grey with morning. She was researching different kinds of poo and what they meant. The colours and consistencies, the signs that meant you had to go straight to the hospital. She peeked inside the layers of clothing, tried to see if it looked more brown or green. What if she was dehydrated? Under the chair, a skitter of claws. She reached down and picked it up. The mouse cowered in her hand. Its twitching whiskers mirrored her fears.

A light flicked on in the house opposite, followed by speckles of water against the mottled window. Someone was getting up, having a shower. They were probably going to work. She plotted the course of her old morning routine – the coffee cup she balanced on the bus, the jam sandwich eaten at her desk while she read over the first emails of the day.

'I know you're there.' She could see a dark shape under the coffee table.

One step, then another. It watched her suspiciously.

'It's me, isn't it?' She cradled the longed-for head against her hot skin. It had taken so long to get pregnant. All the tests, the hormones, the bloating before she was 'harvested' that made her feel like a frog swollen with spawn. The pain, the wait for viable embryos and implantation. Such yearning for this person that she hadn't realised what she needed to lose in order to care for it. Herself. All of it had fallen away, everything she'd built over the entire span of her life fractured and split under the weight of this fragile thing.

The first dregs of light came through the window, touching the feet of the grief tortoise.

Gayathiri Dhevi Appathurai

Gayathiri Dhevi Appathurai has an Engineering degree in Electronics & Instrumentation and works in the Information Technology industry. She is a trained Indian Classical Carnatic musician and has performed in renowned fine arts venues in southern India. Her other creative pursuits include sketching, painting and sculpting. She lives with her husband in Mumbai.

Donut, Paper Napkins and Hope

There are times when the desperation to sustain a livelihood would far outweigh anyone's perception over how it's earned. My body injected into a giant ballooned up donut, dancing and waving at giggling kids and adults, sometimes annoyed office goers, in the middle of one of the busiest roads in Mumbai, could qualify as one of those times.

My family of four makes their meal plans on the one hundred rupees I earn on a day as a giant donut. Eighty rupees if you take away my commute. I try not to eat too much during the day, two bananas are heavy enough for my body and my pocket. For a scrawny nineteen-year-old who cannot lift anything beyond an inflated balloon, I am happy I found this job.

The owner of the shop is a good man. A bit temperamental, but kind, nonetheless. He knows that I don't add customers with my costumed act, but he pays me to come, every other day and weekends, sometimes to double as an unofficial security, mainly to steer the street kids away. He says, 'the platform kids' hovering about is not good for business.

Sometimes I think it's the shop's name that is not good for business.

"Go nuts over Do nuts" written in neon color reminds me of a seedy bar in one of the bylanes, at night. I really don't know what the name means. The owner is proud of it, though, he says his daughter named it all the way from America.

It pays for my living. It must be good indeed.

*

Today there is a good swarm of street kids roaming around this area. It is a busy day, and the traffic junction is just a few meters ahead. They carry anything they can find, from toothpicks to earbuds, walking frantically around vehicles hoping to sell them for some loose change. I could very well have been one of them, if my uncle hadn't helped us out. In some ways, I am still one of them. What I do on this side of the road isn't too different from them.

Babu is the tiniest of the lot. He doesn't look older than five. He clumsily clutches bundles of paper napkins, hops around the junction like his own little playground, much to the chagrin of the stressed-out drivers, yells out "Napkin! Napkin!" He even does a little demonstration of how to wipe the face or hands with it. I always smile when I see him do that. The other boys do their bit to persuade the passengers to buy some napkins from him. I am yet to see anyone buy it. But he is never deterred. He skips to the side of the road just in time for green and waves at them as they leave.

Some of the boys with him, swear at the drivers that don't pay attention. Babu just observes. I wish he wouldn't learn those words. He hides around the turn and observes me dancing. He mimics my little dance before his mother drags him away. He knows he is not welcome near the shop; he never breaches the periphery, he is perceptive that way.

*

I pick up my patty stuffed bun for lunch and sit down in the shade. I feel like having something fried today, it fills me up till night. As I enjoy my little splurge, I sense someone teetering around the side. Babu gives me a cheeky grin. His energy is infectious. He doesn't wait for a moment; he sits beside me. I cannot help but smile back.

"Ey, paper napkin! What are you doing here?"

"Me Babu" he proudly presents his hands.

I keep my half-eaten lunch aside and take his tiny hands "me Kiran."

He waits for a second, as if memorizing it and continues "why are you wearing a balloon?"

"It is a donut."

"What is a donut?"

"It is a sweet."

He gives a small yelp and contemplates his next question. Before we could continue, his mother yells out his name. Babu hops up. "I will buy sweet donut" he says resolutely. I nod at him. It may remain a wish for a while, but I don't have the heart to relay that reality to this kid, not today.

*

It is raining incessantly today. The platform is a puddle. The owner tells me to hand out some samples, since I cannot do much else. The traffic is at a standstill. Two of the motorcyclists have parked their bikes and are rushing inside for some sugar rush. A few delivery bikes are stopping in front. Looks like it's a good day in the shop.

Babu and other kids have wrapped themselves in plastic sheets and are going about their business. Babu has tucked his napkins inside his 'raincoat' and walks around purposely. He scopes out his potentials and approaches a bike guy. He almost seems to have a sale, only for the person to wave a hundred rupees at him and Babu doesn't have any change to give back. He frantically searches for his mother, but I can see that she is far away. The driver finally gives the napkin back to him. The look on the kid's face is that of disbelief. He almost had that money. And then he didn't. The traffic moves a bit, but Babu doesn't wave at them. He goes and sits under the flyover, smooths his napkins, starts kicking some little pebbles to a modest distance. Maybe he is having the first taste of reality of experiencing the never-ending gap between what we want and what life gives us. He is young, but he will learn to not expect much from life. Maybe today is the day he discovers the finest recipe to our happiness, no expectations. He snaps up when he hears his friends and other old boys call for him. He jumps up and runs towards them. I guess he is fine for now.

The sky opened up; life is back to usual. The beauty of Mumbai lies in the unrelenting energy, come thundering rain or sweltering heat. I am back in my costume, but inside the shop. We are hosting a birthday party for a kid and his friends. I am serving donuts and the kids are taking turns to punch my costume, their definition of fun. The owner too, finds some humor at me flailing to balance the tray.

The birthday boy takes fun to the next level, takes a plastic knife and pokes into my costume, the balloon deflates with a squeaky sound, I am caught inside, lose my balance and fall down. Amidst collective chuckles and some mild chiding by the boy's mother to say 'sorry', the server at the shop counter helps me up. The little boy looks a bit red faced being caught doing something naughty, so the owner gives him a special donut to cheer him up.

I step out, needing some air and distance from the squealing children. As a stark contrast and a sharp reminder of reality, I see children in the junction, some begging, some thrusting knick-knacks to the passengers in a bid to earn a few rupees. Babu is there too. He is his usual charming salesman. An old couple is checking his napkins from their car. I am nervous for him. Today could be the day he makes his first sale; the scene looks hopeful. As the old man slowly picks up his wallet, I am getting restless, it is just twenty seconds until the green signal. Babu doesn't take his eyes away from the old man. He counts a couple of notes and hands over to him. Babu beams like a million rupees. He runs away just in time for the signal opening up. I can finally breathe. It feels like I earned a jackpot.

I turn around to see the birthday boy is still sulking in a corner. I sigh.

Babu confidently strides across the road and comes towards the shop. It has been three days since his first sale. The counter boy promptly stops him and asks him to step out. As much as it stings to see this, I feel relieved the owner isn't inside right now. The kid, at his age, probably doesn't realize the significance of being poor in the society, he looks at the counter assistant squarely and says, "I want to buy sweet."

He asks him back "Do you have money?" He proudly presents twenty rupees to him.

"I need twenty more rupees for a donut," the shop assistant says. I expect the little boy to feel disappointed, but how wrong I am. Babu simply takes the money back and says, "I will come back later," gives a sideway glance at the donuts on his way back. His gaze stops when he spots a chocolate flavor, and his eyes sparkle for a moment. This must be the one then. He then hops out and joins his friends.

I hadn't seen the kid for a few days. For a while now, the best part of my day is watching him, zip through the crowded traffic like he owns the road. When I see him smiling through so many rejections, it gives me hope to pull through. He is what I hope I could be, money or not. I hope I had the mind of that child, practically unscathed by the maladies and dejections, the unpleasantness that brews for years into a deep-set resentment, a perpetual shadow of defeat that has become our constant companion in life.

I sit down for a break when I see a familiar hop. Babu is walking behind his mother. He seems a bit tired. Maybe he is down with flu, it is not uncommon this season. He sticks to her as she goes around selling. He carries some bundles for her, the bag is as big as him. He sits down under the shade more than usual. He lies on the pavement, curled up, he looks tinier than usual. His mother gives him water and some bread. He sleeps almost the entire day, his mother scoops him up on her shoulder and carries him away. My heart breaks a little.

For a moment, he opens his eyes wearily and waves at his fellow boys before he disappears around the corner.

My owner called me this morning asking me to meet. There is no party in the shop and I don't have shift today, it really makes me nervous. Things have not been good at the shop lately; I keep hearing of pay cuts. I get down from my bus stand and walk slowly. Maybe I could delay the inevitable by a few more minutes. I see that my boss is sitting inside the shop solemnly with some receipts in front. The look on the counter boy's face confirmed my worst fears.

"Kiran, come in," he says, takes a deep breath and continues. "The shop hasn't been too profitable for a while now. I tried many things to revive it, but I simply cannot make any profits at the current rate. I am doing some cutbacks. I will have to let you go. I am doing some free online promotion."

I feel numb. I saw it coming, but not so soon. I nod at him. He gives me two hundred rupees and one small box of donuts as a parting gift. I say my goodbyes and step out. I take in the scene before me, one last time. The crowded junction, tirelessly honking vehicles, some drivers sneaking away during red lights and the street kids working and in the midst of it, little Babu on his charming hustle.

Reflexively I walk across the road, spot his mother and talk to her. She flags Babu down, he flashes towards us. I give him the box of donuts; he looks a bit confused. He tells me he needs another twenty rupees for a donut. I smile and deposit the box with him. He opens it, sees the chocolate donut and jumps joyfully. I wait for him to charge at his donut, but he runs towards the other boys and talks to them animatedly. And starts distributing the donuts to them. They perch on top of the parapet wall and start eating. I feel overwhelmed at the big heart of this little boy.

As I am about to leave, Babu waves at me joyfully and flashes his infectious smile. I smile for the first time today. At this instant, it feels like I am going to be okay. I see this little boy having a mouthful of donut, possibly the only good food he may have for the rest of the day, and smile like he has figured out life; in all fairness, he might as well have. I walk away with a light heart. I am willing to believe, be it a giant donut or a little paper napkin, there is hope in life!

Nina Cullinane

Nina Cullinane is based on the Isle of Wight. She has an MA in Creative Writing from UEA, has taught Creative Writing and done all sorts of arts jobs to support her writing. Nina was a recipient of New Writing South's NWS10 scheme for promising writers in the South. Her novel, currently on submission, has received commendations and been placed in competitions, and her short fiction has appeared in *Litro* online. She is drawn to writing about seaside towns and social conflict, illness, ageing and the ghosts of our pasts. Alongside short fiction, she is working on a second novel.

Miss A Up the Hill

Konnie cannot stand Age Concern and their bloody concern. She told them she could fend for herself, she was in the Land Army, but then they sent Radu with his sinewy arms and his silver car. He works out, she tells the people in town. He reminds her of the boys in uniform going off to war, of bodies glimpsed through crisp shirts, up close at the dances that smelled of Brylcreem and musk and sex; he reminds her of Gordon Summer, who used to touch her in alleyways up against walls, and how she wasn't then touched in anything like the same way for thirty years or more. And how is it that Gordon Summer's love letter is in her hands, the one she's been searching high and low for? She refolds the letter and tucks it inside her bra.

Konnie finds Radu in the kitchen.

Radu on his knees with something on the floor. It's textile, large, floral. Her skirt. He's scrubbing the floor with her favourite violet-print skirt.

She feels herself snap – brittle as a dead twig.

'That's my skirt, you pilfering brute!' she cries, but Radu doesn't flinch, he never does, just carries on, his sinewy arms working backwards and forwards. And later, she finds him ferreting about in her bedroom, whisking past her with the commode bowl in hand. 'What are you doing?' she exclaims, 'I'll get a woman in if you keep breaking into my bedroom like that!'

She's not stupid, she knows what they say about her in the town: *Miss A*, they all say, *Miss A up the hill, who goes through carers like hot dinners, frittering her money away on men from strange countries because no one else will work for her...*

Konnie comes to in the semi-gloom, on the Chinese rug with the smell of dust and the central heating blasting out ten to the dozen. She's not sure how she got here, but there are scraps of memory of the beautiful delinquent from the flat upstairs arguing outside about the parking space, and now her head is groggy and she's aching all over. She can smell the dust underneath her. The Chinese rug needs a hoover. It belonged to her sister, Stasia. Gaudy thing with its swirls and curls; pretentious, just like Stasia was. She inches her way towards the phone, biting her lip and steeling herself to the pain. *Piekna mala rzecz*, her mother used to call Stasia – pretty little thing, while Konnie was moody little thing – *markotny mala rzecz*. Her mother said Konnie's moods would make her a spinster because who would want to put up with those. *Keep up Konnie*, she used to say, *keep up, a*s Konnie dawdled behind. Never that to Stasia, who was always ahead. Stasia always knew where she was going. Oh yes!

Konnie can feel something poking her; something wedged inside her bra. She pulls the envelope out onto the carpet, crisp as greaseproof after all this time, and inspects it in the dim light. *Gordon Summer*. She gazes down at his gushing handwriting, the splodge of ink containing his thumb print like the circles of a tree trunk. The house in the country they'd fantasised about with its troupe of children and animals and birds flying around. Gordon Summer: gone now, dissolved into matter and air along with everything else that ages and dies. *We are such stuff as dreams are made on*, she mouths to herself, *and our little life is rounded with a sleep…*

Oh, the betrayal!

The sharp descent from rainbow colours to black that have plagued Konnie, on and off, for most of her ninety-four years. She thinks of the man in her life now. Radu. Nothing in common with Gordon except for the way he makes her feel out of control, disastrously aflutter… What is it about men that they've always had this effect on her? Perhaps she should have got into women. Her sister had – her sister had got into *everything*. Konnie had been too safe for her own good because where, after all, had it got her? Radu and his scrubbing floors: she could think of plenty of better uses for those arms. Gordon Summer and his hats and slacks, with his big gold watch on his wrist. He knew how to live: how to wring every last drop out of life. He could teach Radu a thing or two.

Konnie puts her hands on the rug and heaves herself along another few inches, knotting her face up at the thudding inside her joints. She can't quite make it to the phone. She holds her hand out to it and stretches as far as she can – it's her ninety-fifth soon, she's sure somebody told her that the other day – she must show them all how alive she is, more alive than a marching band and half an army! She sighs and drops her hand back to her side.

She'd denied herself too much after Gordon Summer; she'd sworn off men for half her adult life; no one like Gordon, nothing remotely to rival the effect he'd had on her. She lifts Gordon's letter to her nose and she can still smell the scent of tobacco and fear mixed in with his musky cologne. She can feel it now, his presence, hanging back, just out of reach.

What do you say Gordon? She wrinkles her nose and peers into the gloom.

❋

Under the scented pergola at her aunt Zenia's, with blue jasmine crawling above her, twenty-year-old Konnie had sat waiting for Gordon Summer to arrive. She'd met Gordon there in Bournemouth the previous summer. Gordon was on leave from the RAF, visiting home, and Konnie made friends with a local girl who'd taken her to the Pavilion where she danced up close with Gordon with the incredible blue eyes, the tall sturdy body and the erection inside his perfectly pressed slacks. What a revelation it had been to Konnie, who'd known nothing of these things, to feel that surge of desire scorching everything in its wake.

And as she'd sat under the pergola at aunt Zenia's waiting for him to return, she'd thought about how this new Gordon, having fought over the skies of France and Germany, would be a different man from the one who'd gone away: sweet, placid, thoughtful. He'd be changed by it, and she'd have to be patient and understanding. She was ready for this: she relished the idea in fact. In his last letter he'd told her how much he wanted to kiss her, and *where* he wanted to kiss her and how glad he was to have found someone he had so much in common with. The big books about the French Revolution and the Russian Empire; the hours he spent tinkering away with mechanical structures that he seemed to disassemble rather than fix. In his father's garage there'd been a thousand little metal parts shining away under the ceiling light, and each time Gordon would explain what they were all for and she would nod and say *yes yes*, thinking about how she would find a way of undressing him and having him enter her hard and silent on the garage floor among the debris without raising the suspicion of the parents in the big house.

And then Gordon had arrived at her aunt Zenia's, and they were kissing each other on the cheek like two perfect strangers. He'd been back at his parents for a week now and was still wearing his blue uniform as if it was part of him. Konnie felt her cheeks sting and her chest constrict; this reserve that had inserted itself where the closeness had been. She'd had a hell of a time getting there at all, she'd been stuck lambing and digging ditches and been forced to invent the lie that her aunt was seriously ill in order to get away; and Stasia already being there at Zenia's for a month now, pruning back the garden and giving the house a full spring clean.

Konnie and Gordon spoke for a while about how things had been for him, and how aunt Zenia had been so kind and invited him to dinner several times since he'd been back. About how delicious aunt Zenia's pierogi were, and how accommodating her sister had been. And it was then that Konnie noticed Stasia, standing at the French doors in the sunshine, watching them with her fawn eyes; her hair in that signature chignon, spindly ankles strapped into patent heels.

'You're going away next week?' Konnie managed to squeak to Gordon, her throat having gone completely dry.

'Yes, but I'll be back,' Gordon said, staring over her shoulder at Stasia, and Stasia staring right back at him.

They'd carried on for a while talking about meaningless things and all Konnie could think about was how he could have died at any time up there in the skies; he could have been blown to smithereens and ended up with the plankton on the sea bed, and she'd have been spared this misery. This! The heat surged into her, and for a moment she was paralysed by it; by the necessity of containing it. She got to her feet, made her excuses, and trudged to her room without a word. She read and re-read Gordon's last letter without a tear. She could feel herself toughen, like molten steel hardening.

✳

So, what an irony, these little appearances of Gordon's in the dusk just as she's about to turn the lights on, Stasia being long dead, the way being clear for them to cultivate the friendship they'd once had. She can feel his presence bubbling up deep within. She can feel it like she used to at the pavilion and on the garage floor with the metal fibres spiking through her clothing into her flesh.

'You've left the door open again Miss A!' the voice calls from the doorway.

'I only leave the door open for you,' Konnie whispers.

'You ok Miss A?' the voice says, moving towards her in the half-light.

Konnie glances up into the orangey gloom. 'I'm ok my darling, I'm always ok.'

The figure comes up beside her, bends down and reaches out a hand. 'I'm here now Miss A.'

Konnie smiles to herself, staring up at him with his dark hair and buzz cut sides. The angular face and striking features. The turquoise eyes that flash at her just as they had that day when Gordon kissed her in the sand dunes, put a hand down her blouse and the other up there.

The streetlights through the bay windows cast patterns across the floor. Konnie gazes at him, her heart thumping and a flush rising in her cheeks. She reaches out to touch the arm he's holding out to her; an arm full of jet black and blood red: of dragons and geishas.

She giggles as he removes her hand from his arm.

'How did you end up on the floor Miss A?'

'There was something about Stasia that you couldn't resist. Sex appeal, that's what they call it. I understand Gordon, I understand.'

Always the beautiful ones, she thinks gazing up at him, always the veneer that throws one off course. Gordon Summer had always had this *power* over her... and so the fall had been more like a plummet, and she'd had to stifle it, to keep it absolutely at bay in order to stop herself from going under. Under no circumstances would she be one of *those* women... one of those piney whiners.

The young man, who has been here before, has given up trying to tell her he's not Gordon Summer but Troy from number three. He peers at Konnie, at her tiny, doll-like body in its strangely rested state on the floor, and thinks about how helpless she looks, to anyone wanting to take advantage, like that Radu guy with his silver car parked wherever he likes.

'I think I might need to call you an ambulance. Don't worry Miss A, we'll get you sorted.'

For a moment Konnie sees Troy, she *hears* Troy. She thinks of the musicality of these modern dialects thrown together in this strange stew of estuary English and a gentrification of the poor that seems to be thrusting all sorts of people up in places you wouldn't normally see them. She thinks about how she would like Troy to lift her off the floor with his beautiful muralled arms and place her in the armchair while he rings for an ambulance, and, when they take her in, as they always do, she will sit in the A&E cubicle making phone calls from the telephone on the retractable unit that you have to purchase a special card to use. And then she sees Gordon Summer again; the blue eyes glinting at her through the dusky light. Eyes that tell her all she needs to know.

❋

Konnie had to watch from the side-lines as Stasia rubbed her marriage to Gordon in her face for the next fifty years, with their two children and the obscene house, the holidays in Monaco and the fancy cars; until eventually Gordon had become ill and died (Parkinson's, care home, slow decline and long, drawn-out death), followed by *she*. Little Miss. Who'd had the long marriage and the lucky death (silent heart attack, blink of an eye; gone).

She'd known all along about Stasia and Gordon's kinky little secret: the so-called friends they'd invite in, the hideous cliché of it all… *it keeps things fresh*, Stasia would say to Konnie, *I do it for him,* which was pure fabrication, she never did anything for anyone that she didn't want to do. And they lined up at their door to oblige; the sadomasochists and the sex pests, because Stasia dished it out and was, as far as Konnie could make out, completely open-minded about what they had to offer in return. Stasia had no idea what it was like to live on rations, to take what little you could get from wherever you could get it. But Gordon was completely taken in, and there Stasia had stayed, hanging off his arm like a coat hanger. And then Stasia had dropped the bomb: that she'd fallen out of love with Gordon after just a few years, but hadn't had the heart to tell him. It was Stasia all over, steal her doll and then fling it out of the pram.

Poor old Gordon, he didn't have a clue, wandering about in his bubble of delusion; fed and watered by the greatest fraud of all, and still that wasn't enough. He'd still desired Konnie. He'd still, after all those years with Stasia, had the cheek to pat her on the arse one Christmas. *You made your decision*, Konnie told him. And she had kept Stasia's secret; because Gordon wasn't the sort of man who'd withstand rejection. Not like the stronger ones, not like she, Konnie, who'd made a fine art of it. What was it that Stasia had wanted when it came down to it? It seemed to Konnie that she had wanted to swallow her up; to void her very existence. It was this Konnie had fought against all her life, and in the end, she'd won. Survival: her greatest achievement.

*

'We always were better suited, you and I,' Konnie says into the darkness. Gordon used to stare at Stasia with those eyes while she was gassing on about this or that, and it was plain to see, he was trapped in love with the wrong one.

Troy sighs and switches on the standard lamp so that he can see something at least. Konnie raises her arms out to him. He gazes down at her button eyes and her pigeon mouth smudged in pillar box red.

'What do you want Miss A?'

'I want you to come here,' Konnie mouths as quietly as if her voice were the breeze floating through the open window.

She puckers up her lips, and waits.

Kevin Donnellan

Kevin Donnellan is an Irish writer and journalist based in England. He became a journalist in order to pursue writing and recently decided to become a writer in order to actually pursue writing. His journalism focused on debunking misinformation found on social media. Kevin's byline has appeared in numerous publications including: *The Times*, *Reuters* and *VICE*. Outside of writing, Kevin has two young children and enjoys running around the Hampshire countryside.

The Hermit

"He who is unable to live in society, or who has no need because he is sufficient for himself, must be either a beast or a god" – Aristotle

I'm going to tell you about the day I moved into my house and how it was a perfect day and how it started with some lad – I don't know who he was – pissing on my head.

And do you know what I was thinking about just before he was pissing on my head? It was five in the morning and I was thinking about a book. My mam read me this book when I was a young lad. It was called Mistletoe Farm Adventures, I think, and it was about these cousins. They were all on this farm. And three of them were proper farmers and knew about hard work and getting the hay in and all that stuff. And the other three were from the city and they were real cunts. And so was their mam. And their dad was alright but he had been in the city too long and he had to go off doing loads of work cause he had lost everything. Anyway, the three cousins from the city – the cunts – they learned about work and farm life and animals and all and by the end of the book they weren't cunts. And sometimes when I thought about the book, I thought maybe all people in cities were cunts and maybe that included me.

I was thinking about that book just before the lad started pissing on my head. And I don't always believe in signs, but I think that was a sign. Because I kept meaning to go into a bookshop and see if they sold it so I could read it again, but I never remembered or I never had money for a book when I did remember. But then the lad started pissing on my head .

If someone had told me someone would be pissing on my head I'd have said Not For Long, I'll Thump The Cunt. But I didn't. I was in my sleeping bag and was all tucked up and the two lads were standing over me and you could tell they were drunk and that they were rich. And one of them started pissing and I could feel a splash and then the other lad said There's Someone Down There. And they started giggling. Not laughing, giggling. It's different, giggling is different.

And I felt like I was paralyzed so I just lay there and I opened my left eye just a little bit but not enough for them to see I was awake. Then one of the lads, the lad who wasn't pissing, said We Should Give Him Some Money and the pissing lad who was wearing red trousers said OK and I could see some notes dropping on the ground.

Then they walked away and I could still hear them laughing – no giggling – and when I couldn't hear them anymore I moved and counted the money and he had dropped 200 quid, just like that, in fifty pound notes. I don't think I'd even seen a fifty pound note before, I'd seen fifty euros loads, but the Brits only used twenties. I was worried that they would come back because they had given too much by mistake so I grabbed my bag and my sleeping bag and I went walking and kind of trotting down the opposite direction towards Southbank.

I walked down to a part where you can get down to the water where there was a little rocky beach and steps if the tide was out. It was six in the morning at this stage and it was September so it was light out and I soaked my sleeping bag in the water to get rid of the piss and I dunked my head in to get rid of the piss from my head too. Then I put my bag on the steps to dry and I sat down. I had four cans the night before because I couldn't sleep and normally that wouldn't give me a hangover, but I think I probably had one because I woke up too early and because it's not a nice way to wake up with piss in your hair. So I sat there and I checked the money again. It was the most money I had since I don't know when.

And I thought I'll go and buy that book later. And then I thought what else will I do with the money? I thought I could buy a tent because some lads buy tents and sleep in them under the bridges on the canals. But they get taken down and broken in bad weather or other lads are at you saying you should share your tent.

Then I thought about the book a bit more. This is why I think it was a sign. There was this lad in it called Twigg. Twigg was like a poacher, he caught animals and fish and all. And he was always up to something. But he knew everything about nature and he sometimes got in trouble with the guards, wait, no, the coppers; because it was an English book. Then there was this other lad that arrived one day and he was a hermit and he had a beard and read loads of books. And one of the city cousins thought this hermit lad was great. And one of the other cousins, one of the farmer cousins, didn't trust the hermit but liked Twigg even though he was a crook. Anyway it turned out the hermit lad was a prick and had been robbing. And Twigg was the good guy all along because he didn't read books or any of that shite. And he just knew where he belonged in life, the country and the fields and all were his home.

Anyway, my mam read that to me and I said I'll Live in the Country One Day and she said You Wouldn't Know Where to Start and I said I Would Know, I Would Be Really Good. She would laugh and say You

Wouldn't Last a Day. But she was only slagging me, she wasn't serious. I don't think she was. And she said she would bring me out to the country one day. And then she died and I lost the book.

And as I was sitting there a couple were walking down on the path above and you could tell from the way they were walking that they were junkies and they had a plan. You can always tell when the junkies have a plan because they're marching down the road like they're too busy to stop. I never say *junkies* out loud, I say *drug addicts* because I remember someone – a man who gives out coffee – saying to me before that the word junkies makes people seem like they're not human and that makes it easier for people to treat them badly and I said to him: That Makes Sense, That's a Very Good Point. But in my head when I see one I still think *junkies* because you can think words even if you don't say them.

Anyway I was staring at them, I can be bad with staring sometimes. And your man spotted me staring and said What The Fuck Are You Looking At? And I said Nothing. And that actually set him off more cause he stopped in his tracks and his missus said Dean, No, Come On and he said No, Hang On, Fuck This Cunt. I just said Sorry and he stared at me for ages and then said Watch Your Back, I Know Your Face. And that was just the worst thing he could have said to me. I felt sick in the pit of my stomach and my breathing went a bit funny and I knew I'd need to get to a jacks very soon because getting a shock like that gives me the runs.

Then he walked away because his missus was at him and they still looked like they had a plan and needed to go off to do it. And I just sat there shaking. I felt sick and worried. And I knew no matter how much I said to myself Don't Be Worrying that I'd be seeing him or worried I would see him all the time now. But there was no point telling my brain to stop thinking about it. I knew I was stuck thinking about it and worrying about him stabbing me or jumping on my head. He looked like someone who jumped on heads. Some other lads on the street were always in fights and talking as if it was just a normal day having someone saying they would stab you, but I don't think I could get used to it. I thought sometimes, maybe if I actually just got stabbed, I wouldn't be worried about it as much anymore. But I wasn't sure that made much sense.

So, I was sitting there thinking about the pissing lad and the scary lad and how I was hungover and I felt A Bit Overwhelmed. I did, overwhelmed was the word for it. That's when I made a Very Big Decision and formed A Plan. I got up and brought my sleeping bag with me even though it was wet. I walked toward Waterloo which made me nervous because that was the direction the scary lad had walked, but I knew I had to be brave if I was to follow through with my Big Decision. I didn't see the scary lad or his missus and I put my sleeping bag in the sun on some church steps then I walked up to the library behind the station and waited for it to open because it opened at eight.

I went to the computers and I went to Google Maps and I looked at it with the satellite thing on so you can see all the green places and I looked for places that had forests and were near to a train station. And I thought I had somewhere picked, but then I remembered I might need to fish so I had to find somewhere else with a river nearby. And that took longer because I needed to read about all the rivers in England and I found a Wikipedia page that had them all. I decided on the River Itchen because I liked the name and it wasn't too far from London and it looked like it had plenty of woods near it. Then I searched for the price of fishing stuff and decided I could catch fish with my hands if I tried for long enough. I asked the library lady if they had any survival books and she said they had two, so I got *How to Stay Alive* by Bear Grylls from the TV and *Scouting for Boys* by Robert Baden Powell from the Scouts.

I asked her about Mistletoe Farm and she said they had it and that it was by someone called Enid Blyton and there were two stories about the same kids on the same farm. So I got both out. And the library woman said Look After Them, OK? And I said I Will. And she looked at me like maybe she knew I wouldn't bring them back, but that she didn't mind because I was polite.

Then I went to a shop called Army Surplus and got a tent for eighty quid. It was a two-man tent and I told the guy I only needed a one-man, but he said it was the best value and that it would serve me well. And he said something about sleeping in parks and I didn't say anything about my plan, but I said OK I'll Take It, so maybe he thought he had guessed right and that my plan was to sleep in parks and under bridges. And then I asked him if he had any cheap rucksacks because I was thinking my bag was probably too small and he said he had just the one and he said he'd give it to me for a tenner, even though I saw it said twenty on the sticker. Between that and the two hundred quid I was thinking This Day is Just Getting Better and Better.

I went and got my sleeping bag back and it was dry already and it didn't smell too bad anymore. I had to find the next train to Shawford which was close to the River Itchen and I checked the train ticket and it was fifty-four quid! And I said There Is No Way I Am Paying That, because then I would only have seventy-two quid left from the pissing guy and the nine pounds I already had before I was pissed on. And I got a bit annoyed for a while thinking about how I'd never had this much money and now it was almost half gone before ten in the morning. But then I pulled myself together and I made A Small Plan.

I waited on a bench that was facing my platform to Shawford and I waited until there was a big crowd going through and I joined them and someone got stuck and the inspector waved them through and then more people got stuck and he waved them through and I went through with them. I was sure he would stop me, but he wasn't really looking. I was shaking going through like I'd just run for miles and even walking down the platform I was waiting for a hand on my shoulder. Then I got straight on the train and went towards the jacks. But as I was going into it – it was one of those big ones with the fancy door like something from a spaceship – I saw a ticket inspector looking at me from the next carriage and I said to myself Oh He Knows Full Well What I'm Up To.

I was nervous on the train waiting for the inspector to come knocking. It took over an hour to get to Shawford because the train didn't leave for a while and I was noticing every minute pass with my nerves. And I was thinking As Soon As This Journey is Over I'll Never Feel Worried Again. And that meant time went even slower because that's how it is.

I waited until the announcer said We Are Now Approaching Shawford until I unlocked the jack's door and who was standing there? Yes, the ticket inspector! And I just nodded at him all casual and stood looking at the door and he waited a second and then said Ticket Sir? And I said Sorry What? And he said Ticket Sir? I've Been Down the Train and I Think I Missed You. And I started fumbling in my bag and said Oh It's Here Somewhere, Hang On. Then the train stopped and the door opened and I said Hang On There, I Have It Here, Where Did I Put It? And he was standing there looking very polite and patient but I knew he was thinking I've Got This Cunt. And I stepped off the train, but was still making a big show of looking in my rucksack and I put my tent and my sleeping bag on the platform and said Hang On, It's Got To Be Here. And I was really worried now and I thought this was the end of the plan and he'd have the police onto me. And he said Are You Getting Off Here Sir? And I said I Am Yes. And he said Try to Keep Your Ticket Close to Hand Next Time OK? And I said Oh Yes, Of Course, I'm Sorry and he just hopped back on the train. I was so relieved and I just walked out of the station, the turnstiles weren't closed or anything.

The walk to Tesco felt long because it was warm and I had to walk on a road without a path and it had loads of cars and I felt like all the drivers were saying Who Is This Fucking Eegit? But I didn't mind the walk because I felt free and relaxed. I wasn't worried about the scary lad or about getting caught without a ticket or about where I would sleep that night. The last time I had felt this good was when I left Dublin for London and thought I would make my fortune. And as I walked, I patted myself on the back for my Big Decision. I said I'm Never Going Back to London, This Is It For Me Now.

When I got there, I bought a Lucozade Orange and sat outside and drank it and it was one of the nicest drinks I've ever tasted. Do you know how sometimes you can have a load of different fizzy drinks some days just because you can and you don't even notice them? This drink was special because I wasn't in London anymore and I had a plan and I knew as I was drinking the Lucozade Orange that I would remember how good it tasted forever.

Then I went into the big shop and bought enough sausages and rashers until I had figured out hunting. And I bought one slab of cans and told myself that I would be careful to only have a few each night. And I bought a big box of tea bags and a big milk carton and a tin for heating things and a pan for cooking and some matches for until I learnt how to make a fire and a big bottle of water that I could drink and then fill again from a river or a spring and a multipack of small

KitKats and a slice pan and a small bag of potatoes and some butter. That came to 30 quid which was a lot for one shop, but I was doing maths in my head as I went and I knew if I spent less the next shop and then less again I would have enough until a few weeks' time when I had read all of Bear Grylls from the TV and could do everything by myself.

The walk to the country from Tesco was tricky and I got turned around a bit, but eventually there was a bit where the hedge stopped and I could see a forest and a bit of the river. It was more fields over from the road than I guessed so I just got over a gate and walked through one field and then another and kind of got stuck in a hedge for a bit and then I got stung by some green things that I think were nettles and then I saw a cow and then I got to the river. Then I walked along the river for a bit, then I left the river and the cow, who was staring at me, and I walked up to where the forest started.

I wasn't sure it was the same forest from the library computer back in London, but I liked the look of it. There were hills all around and it was quiet like nothing I'd heard before. Not just big park quiet. I walked straight into the forest and there was no path, but it wasn't hard to find a way through the trees and I only got stung by a few green things. The stings were sore, but I liked getting stung because it reminded me of being at home and the patch of land behind the community centre where everyone hung around when we stopped going to school.

After I don't know how long, I came to a place that had a nice space between some good trees and wasn't too dark and I said This Is The Spot For Me. And I was going to sit and eat first, but then I said No, I'll Power Through and Get My Camp Sorted. It took ages making a clear space without sticks or stones on the ground and putting up the tent because there were no instructions and I did it wrong twice. But when I finished, I felt really tired but really satisfied and that was a nice feeling. The fire wasn't too hard, but it was very big and I was worried I might burn down the forest, or people would see all the smoke, so I thought I must read about small fires. But my sausages were cooked and I ate them with bread and ketchup and brown sauce and I really think it was the best meal I ever had. I didn't even have a can with my dinner, just the water and it was delicious. And I arranged my sleeping bag and my books and my spare clothes really neatly in my tent and I felt like I could be happy here forever.

Then I started thinking about how quiet it was and that made me worried for a little while because it felt too quiet. And I started worrying about who could find me here. And in London I would probably have grabbed a can to ease the nerves but I didn't here, because I was able to say to myself It's OK, Quiet Is Good. And after a little while I started to believe myself; quiet was good.

Once I was calm, I started to read Bear Grylls from the TV, but then I said No I'll Read The First Mistletoe Farm, Bear Grylls Can Wait. I don't think I'd ever sat and read for that long. The book was just as good – no better – than I remembered. Every chapter had a different story and I knew that it was for children really, but I could still like it because it reminded me of my mam and of how good reading was. Not just reading the free paper in McDonald's but sitting down and reading a book which I hadn't done in I didn't know how long. And all the stories about farming and nature and hard work made me feel full of hope and I must have read half of the book there and then.

Then it started getting dark and even though it was early I said I'm Going to Bed. I even said it out loud because who could hear me but the owls and mice? That never happened in London because I'd be worried someone would stop and bother me. So, I would wait till the rest of the world was asleep before I slept. And every night I had a new home, but none of the homes were my homes, they were just patches of ground where no one was already sitting. And I suppose this patch of ground was also just one where no one was already sitting, but it felt better than that. It felt like I'd found a little window into another world and crept through it and no one but me could find this patch of earth. That's what it felt like.

And sitting in the dark I knew I would remember it as a perfect day because it started with someone pissing on my head and a lad wanting to kill me and me feeling sick in my stomach. Imagine that! Imagine how good a day must be to be your perfect day and it starting with piss in your hair from a lad in red trousers and then getting even worse than that for a little while. I don't even remember stirring in my sleep in the tent that night, I just slept straight through until morning.

Louise Finnigan

Louise Finnigan is a novelist and short story writer. Her work has been longlisted for the Mairtín Crawford Award and shortlisted for the Cambridge and Manchester Fiction Prize. Her story, *Muscle and Mouth*, was published by Fly on the Wall press as part of their 2021 shorts season. She holds a degree in English and Philosophy from the University of Manchester. Her stories are set on council estates, in high-rise flats or cheap holiday resorts and aim to present the complexity of situations and lives that might be easily dismissed as non-literary. She is working on her first novel.

Speck

On our first night the sky clouds orange from where the nursery is burning. But I don't know it's a nursery. Not then, as I stand on the new bed in Rainbow Brite pyjamas with my nose against glass, strangely cold. Mum is taking things out of boxes, watching us watch the sky. 'Just kids,' she says as if that explains it. 'Kids with nothing better to do.'

Everything takes on the glint of fire. The front drive to the left with its scattered motorbike parts, crisp packets, its one abandoned jelly shoe in flamingo pink. The drive to the right with its grey-green nettles and weeds. And our own, in the middle, newly paved. We've never lived in a terraced house before and everything feels squashed-in and strange.

Gem bounces on the bed. Just a little. Just enough for me to notice her and put my head against her feather hair. We hear Mum crushing empty cardboard, a cough from the other side of the wall. We do not hear sirens.

When Mum said the new house was on a jewel carriageway, I hoped for sapphires or emeralds. But there are only kebab shops and dead flowers tied to lampposts. The two boys from the house on the left scream between cars, playing chicken. Their sister comes to hang off the gate, tells me they're going down the bungies to do knock-a-door-run.

'What's the bungies?'

'Where old people live,' she says, tilting her head until she's upside down and level with me. 'You comin' then or what?'

'Oh. No thanks.' My arms are wobbling. I kick down from my handstand and straighten myself, the blood rushing to my face. I take Gem's hand and pull her away.

*

The boys are called Kyle and Nathan and the girl is called Ashleigh. I watch from my bedroom window as she pulls her knickers to the side and straddles a bucket.

'Don't look!' she shrieks, right there on the front drive.

'Kinelle!' Kyle says (because it will be a few months before I learn to hear the word 'fuck'). 'Kinelle, Ash. Your piss stinks of fish.'

When she is done, they take it past the front of our house and up the nettled path next door. I don't understand why they would do this to the man in the house on the right. He's so quiet. 'Wouldn't know he's there,' says Mum on the phone when people ask about the neighbours. 'The *other* side though, let me tell you...'

Kyle and Nathan shout words I don't recognise as they slosh the bucket out over the step where no-one stands, over the door that no-one opens. Ashleigh squints up at the windows, defiant.

*

In the back garden, between the high fence panels Mum has put in, we roll on the itchy grass and suck at lime and cherry ice pops. Our paddling pool is bright with splashy light and our swimming costumes are patterned with pineapples and beach-balls. We play that Gem is a stranded mermaid, and I am a phoenix who swoops down to save her. 'Woooshhhhh!' I say out loud, trying different noises. I flex my shoulders (glancing up at the windows on the left to check for Kyle or Nathan) and scoop Gem against my chest. 'Shhhhhwoooooo…' The mermaid is safely back in the seawater. She lowers her face and starts to drink it.

'No,' I tell her, tucking my wings away and sliding my normal-girl hand under her wet chin. 'You shouldn't do that. Dirty.'

I look at the other window this time. The empty one on the right. But I'm not sure, suddenly, if it is. I pull Gem towards the kitchen for another ice-pop. She is six years younger than me, and I can't play with her forever.

It's nearly my First Communion so I sit on the carpet at school and learn about having specks on my soul. They will be there long after I die, adding years to the waiting room that comes before heaven. The specks don't only come from things like swearing or forgetting to brush your teeth. They are trickier than that. Some of them are almost invisible. I put my hand up to ask how I can stop the specks from slipping in when I'm not looking. I imagine them everywhere like pollen, like flakes of ash on the night of the burning nursery. The kids from next door go to a different school down the road, so they won't even *know* about the specks. I wait and wait until my arm hurts, but they just keep talking about the bread (so clean and perfect, like a white wafer moon) and how it will take all the specks away, all our doubts, all our questions.

It sounds brilliant. I put my hand down.

*

Metal spikes scrape my belly as I try to wriggle under the fence. It drags my skirt up and my legs flap about stupidly, kicking at concrete and air. I shouldn't have come. I should have stayed in the garden with Gem.

'Shell!' Nathan shouts as he stands over me and laughs.

I don't know what he means but it has something to do with embarrassment. Shame spreads through the parts of me that are close to him. Kyle is there too: over on the wrong side, with my legs. I cannot breathe under the spike.

Ashleigh slips, slick as an eel, and yanks at my skirt until it covers me. 'Don't be snide, Nath,' she says, and they snigger and slump away towards the burned things. I try to follow her by sucking in my flesh and pretending not to care about the skin on my cheek as it tears. She holds her hand out as I wobble to my feet. We walk together across the blackened grass.

'Look, that's where the bikes used to be. Under there. And they had a wall you could do whatsit on… you know, thingy.'

'Painting?'

'No!'

We've played out together a few times now, me and Ashleigh. And I'm starting to notice things, like how she gets frustrated over her words sometimes.

'More like…'

'Chalk?'

'Yeah. And them duck things for riding on. It was dead good.'

She nods at Kyle and Nathan who are poking at a yellow shape that has half melted into the ground. The spring that plugs it to the charred floor still has some bounce. They creak it back and forward and stare hard into its faded beak.

'Who did it?' I ask because she seems like someone who might know. But Ashleigh just looks at the floor and says: 'Some nobheads. Some nobheads did it.'

'Yeah.' I try to push those kinds of words from my mouth but can't. I start to worry about the specks. The air must be full of them here.

'Do you think they saw?'

Ashleigh jumps down from the railing, scratches about in the rubble and dust. 'Saw what?' Where her Power Rangers T-shirt rides up, I see deep shadows between each knobble of spine. I wonder if she is hungry and if next time, I should bring something. Hula Hoops perhaps, or Chewits.

'Me. When I was under the fence. And my skirt was up.'

The thought of the window on the right comes, uninvited.

Ashleigh licks a fingertip and rubs at something from the dirt. Something small and glittering. I wonder if it is glass. A tiny splinter of glass from the shattered nursery windows. She is looking at me now, holding it out to me.

'Don't let people make you feel stuff,' she says. 'Fuck 'em.'

I gasp.

'Fuck. Them,' she says, lifting her finger like a gift.

*

What I hear in the dark:

Cars on the carriageway. Some slow like tearing paper. Some slicing at tarmac, leaving wounds in the air.

Gem's cries. Hot and sweaty from the bedsheets. The sigh and shuffle of Mum's feet. How she cries sometimes, about Dad.

Far away, Kyle's video game. Ashleigh's door-slam.

Nearer, on the other side of the wall, a creaking about, and a coughing. When the other noises stop, it doesn't.

*

I make my First Communion in a plain white dress with a peach sash.

'Don't worry,' Mum says. 'People won't get dressed up too fancy around here.'

But the church carpark is crowded with hoops and veils and little white gloves twirling at diamante drop earrings. I feel the guilt of her palm smoothing my hair as I kneel to pray my soul-specks away. The altar has carpet like marzipan and the priest speaks from folded robes of icing. He gives us the moon-wafer then talks for a long time about how we are different now we've received it. We must love one another. We must love our neighbours as we would love ourselves.

I think: *All of them?* And feel the specks sliding in.

I try to ignore how the moon-wafer dissolved on my tongue so quick. As if it was never there.

*

I stay at Ashleigh's house overnight. She has a telly in her room, and she says we can watch whatever scary film we like. 'Chucky?' she offers. Then lowering her voice, 'Or… The Exorcist?' I don't know these films because I only have videos of Care Bears at home but in the end, she can't get them off her brothers anyway, so we just watch TV.

She tells me the names for body parts I shouldn't let boys look at. She tells me about what people do when they're in private and what is normal and what is *not*. I take it all in, feasting on the knowledge until it starts to churn inside me. I have nothing to give her in return except the food I sneaked into my bag from home.

'What's this?'

'Soreen. With butter.'

'Oh.' She wrinkles her nose. 'Nasty.' But she eats it all anyway and falls asleep, mouth open, in front of The Crystal Maze.

'Get out' the team hiss through the tiny windows as the contestant fumbles with the locks and codes. And I think of that cough and the silence that surrounds it.

I don't know if I really remember blue lights on our street in the middle of the night. Voices on that doorstep where no-one ever stood. Nettles green and seething as they took him.

I think Mum used to talk about it when we were meant to be in bed. Clutching at the helter-skelter phone cord, angling her mouth around broken sentences.

'But why would they put him...' 'But in places like this...' 'Turns out people around here knew about him, but they couldn't...' 'Thank God nothing happened to them.'

This will be the most she ever says.

She thought she knew things, my mum. But she only knew the bit of the world she'd been used to. That's all any of us know.

That morning, before my Communion, she asked Ashleigh's Mum to take a photo of the three of us on the drive. I'd never seen her standing in daylight before. She wiped her hands on her leopard print top over and over before touching our camera.

We stand there forever: Mum, Gem and me in my un-shining dress, my simple peach sash. I clasp my hands under the frown of hedges and the sky cut by telephone wire.

The flat-faced houses stare down with empty eyes.

We look so little.

*

This is what I am sure of.

A different day in the garden. Before the blue lights but after the moon-wafer. Gem is having a picnic and pulling the threads out of Mum's best blanket. She is smeared in leftover strawberries.

I am upside down, watching her through the arms of my handstand. I feel the muscles in my arms holding me still and straight. No wobbling, not anymore. I see Gem's face, bright with pulp. I see the high windows of next door. I hear him. A cough. And a click.

I right myself.

'Go inside, Gem.'

And I lift my finger at the pane of glass, at the face I cannot see, at the camera I know is watching. I imagine it shrinking our world into hard little shards of light. Compressing them. Keeping them.

'Fuck you,' I say, just mouthing the words at first. Then louder, rolling them soft and silky over the itch in my lips.

'Fuck. You.'

*

In the burned playground, not too far from the melted yellow duck, Ashleigh is licking a fingertip and rubbing at something from the dirt. Something small and glittering. It might be broken glass, from the nursery. She is looking at me now, holding it out to me. Just a little speck. A gift.

I know I am meant to eat it, so I take it very gently and place it on my tongue. Swallow. It is tiny but sharp. It will grow. It will stay there forever. It will be useful.

David Frankel

David Frankel's short stories have been published in anthologies and magazines including *Unthology, New Short Stories, Structo, Under the Radar, Prole* and *The London Magazine*. He has been shortlisted in a number of competitions, including the Bridport Prize and the Fish Memoir Prize. He also writes nonfiction which has been published in various journals and publications both online and in print.

Sink Rate

Caroline is aware of the sound of a plane's engines, a distant whine on the aural horizon, growing louder, rising in pitch. She has come to the beach to escape the noise of the island's biggest town, but the distant plane is only a minor annoyance. As the sound grows louder, people around her begin to look for the plane in the sky. It is invisible against the glare of the sun until it appears like a sudden mirage, very close, low, moving impossibly slowly.

Holiday makers on the beach pause, phones in hand, to watch the plane descend on its final, tree-skimming approach to the airport's outer marker. Three times a day, six in high season, it is a spectacle that is noted in the guidebooks. Engine noise reflects from the water. She feels the vibrations in her gut. It is impossible not to watch, impossible not to stand hypnotised with the other customers of the beach bar. But today the more experienced among them sense something wrong in the uneven whining of the engines, and Caroline has spent enough time in airports to know that the plane is too low. It wallows in the hot, island air as though it is treading water and then begins a ponderous bank away from the crowded beach; perhaps a rookie pilot misjudging his approach and going around for another shot.

The watchers on the beach freeze as the plane dips lower, then lower still, until its wing touches the water, gently slicing the waves. But this moment of delicacy is an illusion. The pull of that graceful curl of water is enough to pitch the plane violently. Its engines give a final scream and the fuselage quivers. It hits the sea nose first, flipping and lurching into a cartwheel that destroys it in a vast explosion of spray and steam.

Caroline stands with the others, unable to move. It is all over in a few beats of her hammering heart, but those moments seem to have stretched out, filling her past and future. Later she will remember the sound of rain – debris and scattered spray falling back into the sea – and the beautiful rainbow that appeared briefly above the sinking sections of fuselage. She will not remember the smell of aviation fuel or the screaming of frightened children on the beach, although others will. The whole event has taken seconds. It has been captured on two dozen cell phones. A metal tube travelling at 130 miles per hour hitting the water and breaking apart, conceding to the dreadful Newtonian certainty of action and reaction.

For everyone on board, and everyone on the beach, the path of life is altered. She is completely unharmed but Caroline feels this change, although she is only distantly aware of it and won't be able to verbalise it until years later. 'As though,' she will tell her therapist dreamily, 'the points on a train track were switched and the train moved from one line, one set of destinations, to another. The tracks it had been following became more and more difficult to see as the two lines moved further apart.'

In the long moments following the crash, she stands, bare feet buried in the hot sand, dazzled by the sun on the bright sea. The rain of spray falls away and the silence that has closed around her fractures. She becomes aware of voices and screams. Men, locals she presumes, drag small pleasure-boats down the beach and steer them towards the sinking wreckage. Behind her, a drunken Frenchman is speaking in English, trying to sound unimpressed, 'Not the best landing I've seen.' An American nearby repeats 'Oh my God' over and over, speaking into her mobile but giving no indication of a two-way conversation. Oh my God. Oh my God.

The heat of the sun is suddenly too much. Caroline feels sweat running down her temples and her mouth is dry. She feels the sickly sweetness of the cocktails she has been drinking rising in her throat as her entrails churn inside her. She runs, not towards the sea like the others, but to the small toilet block behind the bar where, hovering above the dirty pan and clutching her skirt around her stomach, she empties her bowels.

At the tiny, metal sink, she washes, glad of the cool water. She is trembling. Is this shock, she wonders. Nobody else from the beach is in here shaking. Disgusted at her own weakness she slaps her own face and turns to a small mirror hanging on the far wall. Her image, skin pale and glistening wet, is caught in the small, dirty oval of glass. She raises her hand to wipe it, touching the cold reflection. It is at this moment that she recalls the woman.

As the plane began its final desperate bank and turn, she had seen a single face at a window. A woman's face at the little rectangle of grey glass. In her mind, she replays the moment before the fuselage ruptured. The whole thing had been so close it was possible to see bags being flung from shattered lockers, the colour of the seating. But not people. She couldn't see a single person, she realises, except the woman at the window.

Staring at her own face, reflected in the tiny mirror, she is sure of what she saw. The woman at the window, staring back at her, raising her hand not to touch the glass, but in a wave.

Her hotel is expensive. Gentile beige modernity unfurls from the glass doors and potted palm trees to the counter, elevator and bar area. Her room is large, neat and bright. It overlooks a deserted pool area, empty deckchairs and tables beneath awnings, all surrounded by a high wall. Behind the ornate brickwork is the quayside and beyond that, the blue sea.

On the phone later that evening, her husband's voice seems unfamiliar – that of a person she once knew somewhere else, a long way away. 'Well thank god it wasn't your flight…'

She loses interest in what he is telling her. With the phone clamped against her shoulder, she flips through the pages of her diary. Her finger hovers over today's date and a scribble of altered plans. A chill passes through her. It was the plane she had been booked on before she had been persuaded to take an earlier flight – an opportunity to take some time for herself before the conference, a couple of days in the sun. But, she is un-used to leisure time, mistrustful of it. Her first day had been a tour of the island's unimpressive historical sites: monuments in sultry, cobbled squares and colonial ruins on the hills overlooking the marina. This, the second day, had been for shopping, until boredom and the clamour of the town had driven her to the beach.

Her husband is still talking. 'So what happened afterwards?'

'After what?'

'After the crash?'

'Look, I have to go. I still need to prepare for the presentation tomorrow.'

'Is everything alright, with you I mean?'

'Yes, of course.'

'Okay. If you're sure?'

'Yes.'

'Okay. Bye. I love you.'

'Yes, of course,' she replies, and hangs up.

Caroline always requests a window seat in business class: the same part of the plane she had seen the woman at the window. It's impossible to tell for sure, but the woman may have been in her seat. It isn't difficult to look up a seating plan. Then she calls the emergency number that has been repeated at regular intervals on the news broadcasts.

'Is there a list of those on board?'

'A full list will be released when all families have been traced and contacted. Are you trying to locate a family member?'

'A friend.'

'What's their name?'

'She was in seat five f.'

'And your friend's name please ma'am?'

Later, showered, dressed, make-up re-applied, she goes down to the bar. The chatter is inevitably all about the crash. There is nothing else to talk about.

Almost all of the patrons are men. Almost all are bragging, competing to be the one who was closest to the impact or most involved in the aftermath. A mingling of awe and jealousy are directed towards those who were closest to the action. She takes a gin and tonic to a table close to the bar, content to listen from a distance. The loud posturing of men is territory she is used to, and she finds the bullshit amusing.

A big man in a crumpled but expensive linen shirt turns to her from a nearby table. 'Did you see it?'

She hesitates, considering a lie.

'The crash,' he prompts, as though there could be any doubt.

'Yes.'

'Quite a thing, wasn't it?' He is well into his fifties but his voice is deep, public-schoolish, overconfident in a way she once found attractive. 'I'm Hugh.'

They shake hands and she is drawn reluctantly into the dissection of the afternoon's events.

'I was on the beach when it happened,' he says, with a forced gravity that makes her want to laugh. She doesn't remember seeing him amongst the others, but to her surprise, she remembers very little about the afternoon, other than a meandering walk back to the hotel. Her memory of the event itself is like a video camera knocked out of focus and swinging about in a sweeping blur of imagery. Only occasionally is there a moment of clarity, a sharp detail: the men dragging boats down the beach, the roof of the aircraft peeling away, the woman at the window.

She lets him buy more gins while she listens to those around, all talking loudly, filled of a nervous need to explain, or to exorcise. The back-and-forth of the conversation rattles around her, although she barely hears it. When Hugh's attention falls back on her, she asks,

'You said you were along the beach from the bar, more or less as close as I was, maybe closer?'

'I guess so.'

'I have a question.'

'Shoot.'

'Did you... were you able to see anyone? On the plane I mean, through the windows, or when it... Do you think you could see them well enough to recognise them?'

'No way. It was too far away and moving too fast.' Seeing her face, he adds, 'You didn't know someone who was aboard her, I hope?'

'No. Nothing like that...'

'Well, let me freshen your glass.'

She takes her drink out to the pool and the noise of the bar slips away. Staring into the glistening surface of the water she can recall with absolute clarity how beautiful the plane looked in the moment before it broke up, with the sun bright on its fuselage, its wing tip about to touch the bright membrane of the sea's shifting surface. The smooth carapace of the silver hull gave no indication of the events that must have been going on inside. These things would be spoken of later, at inquest hearings, in the testimony of the survivors. They will play the cockpit voice recordings full of indistinct shouts and electronic voice warnings: *Sink rate. Sink rate. Terrain. Terrain. Pull up. Pull up. Terrain. Terrain.* For now, she imagines the panic of those last moments – a slowed down world – in which the woman in the window seemed to see her, recognise her, and wave.

She is exhausted but can't sleep. There is a current running through her, as though the percussion of the plane's disintegration is still vibrating through her body. She lies on her bed in the flickering light of the television. The only channels in English are news channels. They are interested in only one subject. Other events, a coup in central Africa, another right-wing American talking about immigration, industrial disputes, are bumped down the order and get only a brief mention at the end of each news segment. Meanwhile, interview after interview asks the same endlessly re-formulated questions: causes, terrorists, pilot error. Experts and technicians, less dramatic in their demeanour than the salivating news-jockeys, suggest something more prosaic: there are six million working parts on a modern airliner. Computer generated simulations of what happened are intercut with footage captured on mobile phones. Already, the plane, Sunworld Airlines Flight 458, has become known by its call sign, Sunny 458.

On her laptop, she watches footage of the crash, uploaded from phones. She replays them, freezing the picture, searching for faces at the windows of the plane, squinting at the blurred, low-res images of the shattering fuselage. She pictures the plane as she had seen it in its final moments, counts the windows, looks again at the seating plan. She is certain – as certain as she can be – the woman had been in her seat. On a clip of footage shot from the beach, she sees herself. She freezes the picture. In it, she is staring out, still holding her drink, smiling slightly as though she is watching a performance of some kind. Was that the moment when her eye had met those of the woman at the window? What had it been like for her? Had she looked out, away from the panic unfurling around her, over the tropical sea, blue and still, the white sand of the beach, so close. Had she seen that little glimpse of paradise and imagined that things would be okay after all, because the plane was moving so slowly by then and the ground was so close, and a landing seemed possible after all as, somewhere in the noise behind her, the cabin crew shouted. *Brace. Brace. Heads down. Heads Down. Brace.*

When she finally sleeps, it is with the crash simulations quietly playing on the television. Electronic voices invade fleeting dreams before she falls deeper, away from the waking world. *Sink rate. Pull up. Sink rate.*

The morning is bright and breezy. She takes a cab. The taxi driver's eyes linger on her a moment too long. She slides across the seat, out of his line of sight.

'Town centre, please.'

'City.'

'Sorry?'

'City centre. We are a city.'

It doesn't feel like a city. She could walk across it in half an hour. The taxi is an extravagance.

She steps from one air conditioned environment to another. The conference centre is glass fronted, flags lining the pavement outside. In the foyer, service staff are dismantling tables. At the doors to the auditorium, an apologetic civil servant informs her that the conference has been cancelled. A number of the lead speakers were on Sunny 458. He smiles sympathetically and, on behalf of the Municipality and the Conference Centre, offers condolences for any colleagues she might have lost. Only when Caroline leaves does she realise that she has left her presentation materials in her hotel room.

She wanders through the central district. Most of the businesses are closed as a mark of respect and the main street is unnaturally quiet. On the quay she pauses, staring out across the sea, and thinks of all the distant cities full of people who are oblivious to the fate of Sunny 458. She recalls a bar – Singapore? Hong Kong? – Yes, maybe it was Hong Kong. Dark, no windows, but expensive. Catering for businessmen and women on stop over: people passing through. People still living in other time zones, gathering to drink Martinis at 10am local time. Frequent fliers, like her, never engaging with the locals, never having time to equalise to the pressure of their surroundings, getting drunk, dancing, enjoying liaisons that would not be mentioned in jet-lagged phone calls home. For those people, and billions of others, the news of a faraway plane crash was, at most, a passing moment of interest glimpsed on a TV screen while they made breakfast for the kids, queued for the bank, or sat in a bar drinking beer and eating pretzels.

At a newspaper stand, she pauses. The front pages show photographs of bodies laid out under sheets in a large room – a community hall or gymnasium. She can understand neither the headlines nor the captions, but she wonders if the photographs have been taken illicitly. They are invasive, as though the people in them have been filmed by a stalker as they slept.

The bodies are laid out in precise grids and each has two sets of numbers, one of which, she realises, are seat numbers. They have been arranged according to the seating plan – the matrix that decided who lived and who died. In the rigid arrangement of bodies there are gaps. Spaces left by the ones who refused their place amongst the orderly lines of their fellow passengers: the living. She thinks of the woman at the window – tries to work out where she would be. It is strange to think of her lying with the others, close enough that they could reach out and join hands with one another, as though the shrouded figures have chosen to lie together. These people, strangers in life, have been united in death: 'the victims', 'the dead', 'the passengers of Sunny 458'.

Caroline is thinking of this as she steps off the curb and is nearly run over by a speeding jeep. It dodges around her, horn blaring, as she jumps back. Shaking, on the pavement, she gathers herself, tucking her hair behind her ears and adjusting her sunglasses. Cautiously, she crosses the road and sets out towards the airport, even though it is hot and the terminal is two miles from town. Along the airport road, there is a line of cars, and when she reaches the single storey terminal building she finds a small crowd has gathered there.

Inside, people wander around dragging suitcases. The airport, they say, has been closed to non-essential traffic for twenty four hours to allow investigators and emergency teams to fly in. The departures board confirms this. Back in London, the arrivals board will be showing incoming flights arriving from all over the world – Calgary, Basel, Dresden, Nice, Seoul, Jeddah, Oslo, Hamburg, Stavanger, Sofia, Los Angeles – but not from here, not today. Boards in other airports would announce cancelled departures. Connecting flights would be missed, delayed. A minor airline somewhere will ground its entire fleet of A320s for routine maintenance. The share value of Sunworld Airlines will tank, only to rally again later in the year when fuel prices fall. A web of minor consequences and electronic impulses fan out across the globe, dissipating, becoming lost as they are swallowed by routine and business as usual.

Caroline watches the people around her, wondering who they are, why they're here, if they know how strange this place is. She feels as though she has been cast adrift: no longer here on business, nor is she here on vacation. She is just here, moving through the day-to-day of island life without a reason. To the world around her, she is irrelevant, and for the first time in her life, Caroline feels invisible. On her phone – switched off since the previous evening – messages and emails are silently stacking up. At home, her husband and daughter are going about their lives as though she does not exist. They are as used to her absence as she is used to theirs. She is due to fly back to them in two days, what would have been the end of the conference, but she feels the world slipping away from her and for a moment she considers staying here, floating, half-way between two continents. It is a fleeting thought. When a list, taped to a white-board, tells her that her flight home is one of those that will be rescheduled, she is filled with a sudden panic – an urge to get home that goes beyond the usual yearning for rest and the familiar.

Around the airport's only information desk, uniformed personnel with clipboards are answering questions from anxious customers. It takes time to get to the front.

'I need to get home.'

'We're so sorry for any inconvenience caused by recent circumstances. We're making every effort to re-establish normal timetables. Please contact your airline directly to find out about flight alterations.'

Caroline begins to move away, but turns back to the desk clerk. 'Could you help me with something else? I know someone who was… She was in row five, seat f.'

'Their name please, ma'am,' says the clerk

'Five f. Please check. It's very important.'

The clerk hesitates, but seems to yield, looking down at his monitor, scrolling through a list. She watches the pupils of his eyes as they move, searching rapidly down the screen in front of him. 'Five f was empty ma'am.'

'Empty?'

'Yes ma'am.'

'Do you have a list of passengers?'

'No, ma'am. If you give me your friends name…'

'I… I'm not sure.'

'Not sure?'

It is clear from the clerk's changing tone that he suspects her of something: perhaps of being a reporter, or just a ghoul.

'You should go please ma'am. That information is for relatives only.'

His hand moves towards the phone, perhaps a threat, but she is already turning to leave.

She steps through the glass doors and into the sudden heat of the street outside. Standing beside the terminal, she watches the airstrip through the security fence. The angled shadows of airport buildings point across a neat strip of lawn to the tarmac and sweeping geometry of the taxi-way.

On the apron, a plane is taxiing to a halt. The din of its turbines resonates through her body. Inside her, the vibration feels like fear. She feels a tremble running through her that matches the lowering pitch of the engines as they wind down.

Beyond the airport, across the scrubland at the end of the runway, a small armada of boats and floating platforms have assembled at the crash site. The area of the salvage operation is taped off, as preparations are made to raise the larger pieces of wreckage from the shallow water inside the reef. On the beach, the Minister for Commerce and Tourism, ashen faced, surveys the scene and addresses the press. Later he will attend the nearby resorts, shaking hands and listening to the complaints of outbound tourists whose flights have been delayed, and hotel managers who fear a downturn in visitor numbers. For a generation the island will be remembered as the scene of a tragedy. None of this matters to Caroline, or to the world across the ocean.

Out on the tarmac strip, the plane is still. Ground crew move towards it at a leisurely pace, conserving energy in the heat of the morning. Caroline watches the aircraft. It is a hundred feet closer to her than Sunny 458 had been when it hit the water, but from where she stands the windows are nothing more than small black smudges. Even at this shorter distance, she realises, she is unable to see through the dark bubbles of glass.

Caroline closes her eyes against the dust stirred up by the jets, swirling in vortices in the hot breeze. The air is thick, and the smell of baked earth and engine fumes fills her nostrils. The dying whine of the aircraft engines and the heat of the day folding around her, squeezing the air from her lungs, carry her back to the beach and the sweet, sickly taste of a pineapple cocktail caught in her throat. She can see the rainbow hanging in the spray above the sinking wreckage and the woman in the window breaking apart with the fuselage, dissipating in the shimmer of heat and fumes, leaving no trace of herself.

Gonzalo C. Garcia

Gonzalo C. Garcia is a Chilean writer and Assistant Professor in Creative Writing at the Warwick Writing Programme. His first novel, *We Are The End*, was launched in October 2017 with Galley Beggar Press and was nominated for the Edinburgh Festival First Novel Award 2017. He is currently working on his second book and teaching Creative Writing.

Unlikely Goals Worth Pursuing

I n place of Molly's desk there was now another ping-pong table and a free smoothie bar. And by the basket of plastic oranges and bananas was a cardboard cut-out of a rainbow, each colour matching the available flavours. I picked up an Orange You Glad I Said So and sipped it slowly back at my desk, thinking of Molly. She'd taken charge of the Envisioning Division on a Monday and quit by the end of that same week. It annoyed me that no one mentioned just how much work I'd have to do to cover for her, starting with the rewrites of our group Mood Board and Short-Term Wins. And then the most important presentation of the year, the Unlikely Goals Worth Pursuing, had somehow also trickled down from her desk to mine.

The presentation would take a month to organise and I had to cancel the holiday I'd booked for myself and Anna. It wasn't going to be your typical summer outing either. I'd reached twenty-five years with the company and under its Hanging By A Thread programme we were going to go to the jungle near the Panama Canal to learn to weave waterproof baskets from the natives. But after Molly left none of that could happen. To make things worse, the only presentation prep she'd done was hiring a team-building drum circle, but *Dare To Snare* would only sign the contract once the other guests confirmed. Anyway, I didn't tell Anna straight away. She'd booked time off at the advertising agency where she worked and even bought a new two-piece swimsuit, India Yellow apparently, and I swear I'd never seen her so happy.

"Hey, you hear about Molly?" Sergio said, stretching himself over the open plan desk towards me.

"We all make our decisions. She was a good employee."

"Have you really not been on it yet?"

He looked at my computer screen. I had two windows opened. One was an unsuccessful attempt to cancel the Panama holiday and the other was an ongoing search for a videogame addiction clinic. "Your son's gonna end up a loser," Anna would usually say after drinks on date night. Sonny had finished high school more than five years before but all he ever did was play videogames. Sergio says that when your kid is losing at life they will cry for help in unexpected ways. Anyway, we couldn't afford any of the places I'd found at the time, not any of the good ones, and we wanted the best for him. Nothing but the best would be enough. And so I wished Sergio would let me work, or even better, notice that I was working hard, as a concerned parent, working out of love, Love-Work, as I'd written on our group Mood Board behind the burger stand.

"I'm not interested," I said. "Keep your head down. That's how I got to twenty-five years. Distractions get you into all sorts of trouble."

"None of it matters anymore."

"Of course it matters."

"Look," he said, moving closer, his hand taking over the keyboard. "This is the page."

It looked like a webpage from the 90s: blocky text, underlined blue ad links, blurry GIFs, the low-res spectres of forgotten memes. The webpage had no options, no words. In the middle there was a search bar.

Sergio wrote his full name on it. The screen showed lists of matches. "It's all I've ever written to anyone, about everyone."

"We should get back to work," I said, hoping he wouldn't look for me.

"And if you add a comma after a name and then add someone else you can see what they've written to and about one another. I'm telling you, the world's changed."

Despite Sergio's insistence that the world had changed, that Friday ended in much the same way as they always had, and besides that conversation, Molly was never mentioned again. Her nametag and Personal Growth Table were removed during the weekly lunchtime fasting meditation session at the burger stand. I'd also add that she was not, as I previously mentioned, a good worker. Oftentimes I would say hello and comment on her Personal Growth Table and she'd laugh or roll her eyes with a sigh.

"You've been working here for too long," she once told me.

"I wish it were even longer," I said out loud, hoping Sergio would hear. He was my boss at the time before I caught up and then surpassed him. Then, pointing at her Personal Growth Table: "Did I ever tell you that your Ho'oponopono is off the charts? The secrets of Hawaiian forgiveness, am I right? You're almost in Bloom."

"Suit yourself," she said. "Hope your kid's doing better."

She was always nosying around too, so I wasn't very surprised to hear that others on the Envisioning floor had been writing to each other about her. Even if she only had a few more seminars to run to be in full Bloom, you do always get what you put in. And

I'd also add that you also get what others think you put in. She wasn't putting in a lot. It's that simple. She deserved very little. And that's fine. It was a Positive Lesson, after all, and if she were still at Envisioning she wouldn't have learnt it. That's how the Earth spins, she herself once said at a seminar, it spins on the gravity of our lessons to each other.

And so, having had a normal successful Friday, I went home and was surprised to find Anna smoking on our balcony. Sonny didn't greet me either. He was playing videogames in the living room, like he was not ashamed, and he didn't even flinch when I closed the front door much harder than was necessary.

"Why are you smoking again?" I asked her. She was holding onto the railing, flicking ash to the balcony just below us. I'd have to later go and apologise for her again. She looked at me but wouldn't answer, not even a nod.

"I got fired," she said after a few puffs.

"What happened?"

"Remember back when Duck wasn't my boss? Back when he was just a little Duck? A duckling?"

"Yes, Duck. Very nice guy." I'd only met him once, at a work dinner. He ate caviar with a straw, said it wasn't that big a deal to him, just comfort food, that his whole family were caviar-mad, that it was the first thing he ever ate. Duck gave us some to try on Sonny, to get him used to the taste of success early, but he ate it with a knife and fork.

"Did Duck fire you?"

"Do you remember what I told you about him, about his new haircut?"

"The mullet?"

"Yes, yes, the mullet."

"What of it? It seemed to me a perfectly good mullet."

"I had sent an email to Alfred, you know, Sad Alfred from legal, only guy who talked to me when I started work. Well, it was... no I... I asked him on an email whether he thought Duck could hear us when we spoke, given the party going on in the back of his head."

"You're a bully, mum," Sonny said, watching Mario fall off a cliff on TV. He stretched himself with a sigh. "Being sad is not funny. You're the bad people here. You think you're the good people but you're not. You're the bad people."

"Sonny, he introduces himself that way: 'Hi, I'm Sad Alfred.' He thinks it's funny, so what am I supposed to do, change his name? His identity? Would you like that done to you, Sonny?"

"So they fired you for what, exactly?"

"Have you really not seen the page yet?" she asked.

"No, I haven't," I said, a little annoyed by then at the urgency with which everyone spoke about something so unproductive.

"Well, Duck did. Saw my emails and everything."

"He fired you for mocking his hair?"

"Well, the chain did get a little nastier. More people joined in and everything. It wasn't just me. But then Alfred suggested we kill Duck. As a joke, you know, for bullying him all these years and making him hate himself. It was a joke though."

"I checked the page too, you know?" Sonny said. "You should thank me I haven't left yet."

There were brown envelopes on every desk, even on those which had already been emptied. Inside was a letter.

DEAR u1671643

It is an assumed fact of life that you have by now heard the news about the website. We would never ask you not to read something out of office hours (sadly, we cannot be with you to take care of your business at home too), but we kindly request that you do not check the site, and especially that you do not look for any names of those of us in upper management. We would help you in this endeavour but none of our traditional filters work, believe us we have tried them all, and so the website is still very much visible. Again, this does not mean that you should look – you must not. Looking is not a Positive Lesson. We hope you understand that since we are at the top, we are fewer (remember what we always say, that fewer people fit at the mountain summit), and so we have a lot more to lose. Do not worry, you will not be getting any more work as a result. Some of you will be getting less work, others no work at all! Jokes aside, all this means is that we are sadly forced to check your names on the website so that we can get to know you better, to ensure that we are still a good fit and that you are all a strong base that can support the mountain.

The Summit.

*

A day after the note, Sergio didn't arrive to work – all of his things were gone apart from a picture of himself as a child at his own birthday party, which I always thought pleasantly sad and nostalgic, if a little grotesque because age had changed him beyond recognition. I put the letter back in its envelope and got back to work on my Unlikely Goals presentation.

I was alone on the Envisioning Team floor for a couple of days after the letters. I was glad I had my own cubicle because those who'd upgraded to Open Plan looked the loneliest sat by themselves on long empty tables and going through their morning slides on the projector, laser pointers on pie charts and animated tables even though there was no one to present to.

But not long after, I heard fast typing from the cubicle opposite mine. I ignored it at first, not wanting to appear bothered by the natural sounds of the office but the clatter got so loud I got up to show my disbelief. It was a woman I'd never met. She was wearing headphones and hadn't heard my knocks on our shared cubicle wall. I stood up and went round to her, tapped her on the shoulder from behind.

"Can I help you?"

"Yes. Isn't this desk meant to be empty?"

"I got a letter ordering me to move to Envisioning. Was told you needed the help." She shook my hand. "Nice to meet you."

"So what's your name then?"

"You can call me…" she searched around her desk and finally pointed at the clock on the corner of her computer screen. It had just turned one. "You can call me One."

I returned to my desk and updated my Mood Board:

1) TODAY I feel <u>negative</u> because of <u>personal reasons.</u>
2) TODAY I am thankful for <u>rare moments of silence.</u>
3) BY THE END OF TODAY I will achieve <u>Unlikely Goals Worth Pursuing presentation progress.</u>
4) DARE to <u>Love-Work Harder Every Day</u>.

Click. Share.

One didn't bother me so much once I got used to her typing (though I still thought it was too fast to be done correctly) and I felt guilty for days about my Mood Board entry. We didn't talk save for the morning briefings and to ask each other whose turn it was to pay whenever the doughnut cart passed by. I even forgot she was there sometimes.

But then one day, after an hourly stretching session, I caught a glimpse of an open document on her computer. I couldn't read the tiny writing but managed to make out that every sentence was a bullet point, and that they all had a time stamp at the right edge of the page. From then on, I made sure to halve my stretching time and lunch hour and stopped asking her whose turn it was to get a smoothie and instead resolved to always get it for her. The Summit would surely have meetings about it, my progress and commitment to the climb, the details of my schedule, the value I added, the type of person I was, if only they looked for me on the webpage and found that *our* Short Term Goals had become *my* Short Term Goals, that *they* Envisioned what *I* Envisioned too, and that each time One typed I breathed the kind of relief I imagined reserved for those who, concluding a great climb, get to see nothing but sky above them.

Sonny's first day of digital rehab went smoothly. He signed the care agreement form which meant he'd be there for at least a month. He and all the other digital addicts would go on excursions in the hills just out of town, learn to light fires using only two stones and to meditate in its glow. They also teach patients how to ask someone out on a date. That's the part that convinced Sonny – he just stood there flat-faced when we told him about starting a fire but lit up himself when we mentioned girls and camping. He said he was ready for the next step and we were glad because it was the only time this digital rehab clinic – one of the best, if not *the* best – had ever had discounts, as many people had dumped their smartphones when the website first showed up.

And so it was just Anna and I and the now available TV. She watched the news all day. TV anchors spoke over lines of text panning slowly, blurred out boxes where people's names would have been. I'd come home that day to find her still in pyjamas.

The Pope was seen forgiving all
Your bad text messages
The only good people are long dead
Who would have thought
It was better not to write anything at all?

"Can you believe these bastards?" is how she usually greeted me. She was slumped sideways on the couch; Sonny's favourite fleece blanket up to her neck.

"What happened?"

"Somehow, mysteriously, the messages of all these elite asswipes disappear, just like that – " she moves her shoulder enough to raise the blanket, " – and this sack of shit is now telling us it was a good thing that this happened because it's made us safer and more honest, that it's teaching us how to be more positive in life. Bet you these fuckwits never worked a day in their lives. Easy to be positive then, isn't it?"

The TV anchor was now interviewing a tech millionaire in what appeared to be either a large underground parking lot or an empty gym because there were both cars and bench presses arranged in pairs in the background. I recognised him from a Neat Talk about Making It but couldn't remember his name.

> That was me sending rockets to Mars
> Exploring the botanical possibilities of sand
> Some loser's out there working a job they hate
> Even planets need motivation
> All it took was wanting it
> You can't feel bad
> For being great

I made dinner for Anna and locked myself in the study to do more of the presentation. It had four components, and they each had to be perfect:

IDENTIFY UNLIKELY GOALS

One was very different to Molly. She knocked on our shared cubicle wall and told me it was her birthday, that she'd spent it, quite happily, filling her new blank Personal Growth Table. I commented on it, said that if she tried a little harder, I was sure she'd be in Bloom in no time, by the end of the year even. Instead of laughing in my face or telling me to *look, just do one* like Molly used to, she wrote *bloom* as her first bullet point, her main goal.

I went to get us a fresh Mint To Be from the smoothie bar later that day and was surprised to find that they were no longer free. I only had money for one, so I got hers and got an empty cup for myself. I had to make slurping sounds, fake stir with the straw. We didn't talk again but when I collected her cup, I saw her take notes on the computer. There were many more notes than usual that day. The first word was *Up*.

EVALUATE WORTH

Days later, Sergio called.

"I'm not doing so great," he said.

"We can meet some other time, if you'd like, but I can't talk during work hours."

"I lost my car and I'm biking everywhere now." He was drunk and breathed real loud at the end of each sentence.

"It's good for your health."

"I miss it, man, I miss everyone in there… I miss my desk. I want my picture back. You have my picture? You know, the one of me as a child? I miss that too."

"Your desk was emptied, though."

"Tell me, who's there? How is everyone? Who's there with you now?" I could hear One on the phone to a client.

"It's only two of us now. Someone new."

"I saw Molly the other day, remember her? She's not doing so well, man. She sells swimming pools so she has these mad red eyes and she has to wear sunglasses all the time. Well, she talked about you and she said, well, they'll get rid of everyone someday." One hung up the phone and yawned.

"She's jealous," I whispered.

"She said, 'I'm not jealous,' so I don't think it's that. She said that the only thing worse than appearing on the webpage was not appearing at all."

The conversation left me exhausted the whole day and I was glad to receive news from Sonny. He'd learnt to light a fire and recognise directions from looking at the stars.

1) TODAY I feel <u>positive</u> because of <u>personal reasons.</u>

2) TODAY I am thankful for <u>an excellent co-worker.</u>

3) BY THE END OF TODAY I will achieve <u>Unlikely Goals Worth Pursuing presentation progress.</u>

4) DARE to <u>Trust the Good Signs.</u>

Click. Share.

The elevators in the office had an astrological display of dimmed yellow bulbs simulating the kinds of real-life constellations Sonny would be learning about. I'd left work at the same time as One that day. She nodded with a smile as she came into the elevator and then turned to face the door. We both looked up at the display of lights.

"Orion," I said.

"My name's Lucy," she said, and then the doors opened to a dark parking lot.

PLAN TO PURSUE THEM

Anna got hooked on Sonny's videogames. She said she never wanted to work again, not with the complete lack of motivation that was the fault of whoever had started the webpage.

When I got to work that morning, one of the drummers from *Dare to Snare* was waiting for me at the lobby. He had one of their signature Hawaiian shirts on and a snare drum hanging from his shoulder with a strap. I told him none of the other guests had confirmed yet, but he said the webpage had split the band and he needed the gig. He had talked to someone in the office already. She said she wanted to audition him.

"Have you lost anyone to the webpage yet?" he asked.

"I've not used it."

"Right on."

Lucy and I spent the rest of the day auditioning him and printing I CAN'T DO IT papers for the audience to tear up at the climax of it all. Once we were done, we had Mango Tangos and exchanged ideas about the best possible seating arrangements to make the convention centre look full.

"Sit people around tables," she said. "It will feel more exclusive. The fewer per table there are, the more important they'll feel. If they end up alone it'll be like getting promoted." I agreed and took notes. "Separate them together," she added, which I then wrote on a sticky note next to my Mood Board.

SUCCESS

His best beat at the presentation was

pm pm po-wer	*pm win win,*
pm pm po-wer	*win win win*

which stayed with me long after it had ended. Everyone stomped and clapped to it. I wanted to celebrate the end of the presentation but when I got home Anna was gone. She'd left a note.

Hey,

So, I looked for you on the page, sorry, okay? But all I found out was that you do exactly what you told me you did. You were so goddam mind-numbing, stretching hourly and buying smoothies (what are you, a hippie in rigor mortis?) and you know what, I felt boring just reading about it, you know? I read you were happy that twenty-five years had gone by. You wanted to celebrate it.

I'm more than this. I want more than this. Dunno why I'm writing this, really. I'm gonna go to Panama on my own. I'm gonna weave so many baskets, biblical amounts, there won't be enough water left to fill them.

But first I've gone to visit Sonny. We're gonna learn to make fire together.
xx
Anna
PS. If it's not clear whether I'm leaving you or not it's because I'm not so sure yet. So don't get rid of the videogames just yet.

*

Lucy arrived late the next morning. She was in a better-than-normal mood, even got me a smoothie. We got in the same elevator on our way down to the burger stall at lunchtime.

"It's Orion again," she said, pointing up at the lights.

"Look, I – "

"You're such a good worker, you know? Everyone knows it now, that you're a good, no – and I don't say this lightly – that you're a *great* employee."

We spent the rest of the day brainstorming for next year's Unlikely Goals, starting with the Eidetic Image Method. We closed our eyes. She came up with a mountain-themed stage at a larger convention centre with even fewer people per table and therefore much fuller. She said she'd once seen where The Summit meet, and that every year we should try to be more like that. I agreed and closed my eyes too, but I couldn't picture anything specific. In that weightless moment, almost rising, I considered the infinite possibilities of her full name, the sky above me.

Susanna Gould

Susanna Gould was born and brought up in South London. She studied English and later trained in Theatre Directing. Her career has included work as a teacher, theatre maker and community arts consultant. She was longlisted for the 2020 Mslexia Short Story Prize and is currently working on a novel set in Norway that explores family and creativity

A Mouthful of Nymphs

It was Sophie's suggestion they come up to the roof, but now the boy from Queens is snoring and she can't sleep. It is June. She has been in New York a month. She met the boy from Queens two weeks ago. Tonight they have been at a fancy dress party somewhere in Brooklyn where the names on things aren't the actual names of the things – drug stores are actually bakeries, bakeries are actually homeware stores or hairdressers – and Sophie had to wander around by herself for ages, dressed as a butterfly and in shoes she would never normally wear, in order to find him. Once she found him, she had to pretend not to know him, as per their recent arrangement. A girl they talked to at the party banged on about sleeping on her roof naked and how it made her feel like a bird or a cloud.

When Sophie was six and her father was trying to be a swift, he taught her that the air is crisscrossed by a web of scents, each thread a street that swifts smell their way through. She imagined barbecues and pine and toast. He taught her that the air crawls, that swifts live on the wing, feed from a height, delivered their food on gusts and eddies. He taught her to map this invisible terrain with airborne thistledown and dandelion seeds. Swifts don't come down – can't in fact come down – to rest. When Sophie was a child she heard somewhere that swifts flew to the moon to roost at night. When she announced this with some authority at the dinner table, her father spat out a mouthful of wine. He still teases her about it from time to time, as if she is still six years old.

The insect heat in New York crawls down arms and legs. Sophie is staying in her friend Alice's apartment, which has no air-conditioning. She is supposed to be researching experimental theatre through internships with two theatre companies in the city, but the most productive thing she has done today is watch a tutorial on how to make the perfect raspberry Kool-Aid. Nine cups of water is too many cups of water. It has to be eight and a half. The jug she filled looked like a blue balloon.

Sometimes in rehearsals Sophie is asked to read the lines of a sixteenth century Dutch migrant character. She can't do the accent. More humiliatingly, she has to make the sound of the Dutch migrant's dog. Her father would approve of the task if she told him, would wonder why she found it so embarrassing. On her way to tonight's party, she saw, for the third time, a man on a stationary mobility scooter at the intersection of Fifth and Bleeker holding up a large snake. In the subway on the way home from the party with the boy from Queens, a young man in green sequin knickers danced to music no one else could hear.

On the roof in Manhattan, the boy from Queens moves his hand in his sleep so it touches Sophie's. They met in a bar in Brooklyn and Sophie has slept at his apartment on and off since. She had assumed they were now dating. Macaw-like, he has a knack of repeating back word for word things she has said. Sophie had told herself this meant he was listening, which meant he liked her, but a few days ago he suggested that they pretend to be other people. Or, more precisely, that they pretend they are strangers, always meeting for the first time. Sophie has decided this new, even more casual arrangement suits her better. She moves her hand away from his. A text from her father earlier that evening simply read, "how do swifts connect starlight with chocolate milk?"

Her father had appeared in New York two days ago. It had been a boiling morning in Manhattan. For a moment, iced coffee in hand, checking her phone at the lights, Sophie had felt she fitted. In the park the endless joggers had circled. A group of new mothers had stood in a cluster near the lake, touching their collarbones and fingering necklaces, jiggling small bodies and prams, patting knowingly. Sophie arrived at the Corner Theater's building and, reaching the top of the stairs, standing outside the door of the theatre's office, had heard someone say, "that girl's father is at the deli." She knew immediately which girl.

That lunchtime, the deli was a shock of loud voices, people and cool air. Sophie had tried several times to *Grab-a-Bite!* at the counter there, but each time had failed to get the attention of the waiters, not realising that, in New York, you have to shout your order, and quickly. Her father, though, was sitting at the counter, in his black t-shirt and jeans, as if he sat there every day, despite his gangly frame being too long for the stool. His feet were hooked round the bottom of its legs, his elbows on the counter, like a monochrome flamingo. He was texting with one hand, pushing a sandwich into his mouth with the other. He saw her and gestured, though not at her but at a waiter.

"They're bringing you grilled cheese," he said as Sophie approached, as if continuing a conversation they'd already started. She fixed her attention on the glass of water sweating in front of her father.

"What are you doing here?" Two women about Sophie's age slipped onto the next two stools along the counter and ordered, barely pausing their conversation to do so.

"I've got a conference in Austin on Friday and I thought I'd stop in New York." He gestured for coffee. "I know this place," he added, "good spot."

"Right."

"Do you want to come to the Frick with me tomorrow? I'll sleep this afternoon, but I'll be fine tomorrow."

"I have to work," Sophie said. He was fiddling with his phone.

"It's open ten till four tomorrow," her father said without looking up.

"What is?"

"The Frick."

"I have to *work*."

Sophie's father shrugged his shoulders and drained his coffee, pulled two paper napkins from the dispenser to wipe his mouth.

Back at the theatre that afternoon, Sophie was sent out for iced tea and doughnuts from the stand on the corner of the street. She had left the cardboard tray and greasy white paper bag on the table in the centre of the office and a pile of change on Sandra's desk, and spent the rest of the day drafting and redrafting an email on her phone about her qualifications and abilities, stopping short of mentioning that she's thirty-five, a postgraduate, and should be far beyond being sent out for snacks. On her way home she stopped in one of the tiny community gardens, gems in concrete corners. She smoked her first cigarette, from a soft packet like she'd seen on TV, and hurriedly slipped it back in her bag in case her father should appear there too.

Back at Alice's apartment, Sophie found that the only fan had been taken by the couple Airbnb-ing in Alice's spare room. They weren't even home. The ten-dollar lilac Sophie had bought was making the room tight and headachy, and two bluebottles lay on their backs on the table underneath it, pedalling their delicate legs in the air. She carried the vase to the sink and went to throw the flowers in the bin, holding the mushy stems away from her. She stepped on the pedal at the base of the bin and, as the lid lifted, a shower of plump maggots spilled out onto the floor.

Her father sounded sleepy and confused when he answered the phone. He arrived at the apartment less than thirty minutes later in a taxi. He had befriended the driver and held a card for an Iranian restaurant in Tribeca. "Fuck," he merely said, laughing, on entering the apartment and seeing the kitchen, the floor awash with water and the bloated larvae who, it appeared, could swim. "Where's the hoover?"

After he left, Sophie discovered a pile of twenty-dollar bills in a mug by the sink. The card for the Iranian restaurant was propped against it with a note scribbled on the back saying, "spend me!" She stuffed the card in her bag, pocketed the bills and walked to the corner for ice cream, Kool-Aid and Cheerios, popping a dollar into the plastic cup at the till as a tip for the cashier. That night she dreamt the boy from Queens wanted them to pretend they were horses, fruit bats, oysters.

The day after, Sophie met her father in a diner where she drank chocolate milk and watched him check his email as they waited for the Frick to open. She had texted Sandra at the Corner Theater that morning, making her excuses for not being in the office that day. She imagines Sandra staring at her text and saying to the office "who's Sophie?" and then "oh!"

The Frick was cool and quiet, but this kind of art bored Sophie, the gilt and solid figures. The faces in the portraits seemed to boast of their single-mindedness. A young woman in a lilac evening dress cocked her head knowingly from a painting in the North Hall, two boys dressed as grown men grinned out at her in the library. It seemed to Sophie that her father examined the minute detail of everyone. He struck up conversations with the gallery attendants, seemed fascinated by everything, and oblivious to anything else. They had struck a deal: two hours at the Frick for two hours at The Guggenheim, where, Sophie had read, a conceptual artist had bathed the rooms in light. It took her father twenty minutes at The Guggenheim to declare the delicately changing glow "bullshit" and disappear to the coffee shop on the third floor. "Meet me there when you're done," he had said, turning on his heel.

Once, when she was seven or eight, on the way to school with her father, he and Sophie heard screams in the sky and, looking up, saw a drift of black shapes rising from the treetops. Sophie's father told her to wait in a patch of nettles while he disappeared up a nearby tree. The wet smell of the nettles, the fur on the stalks she knew not to touch, the instinct to look along the ground for dock leaves to rub, in case she touched those stems by accident. She watched her father open his mouth and then spit. Later he told her he'd snapped a mouthful of dragonflies; it was the closest he'd got to becoming a swift. Sophie decided he used "dragonfly" in the same way her grandma used "horses" to describe the foam on the crest of the waves close to shore. Otherwise she knew the image could haunt her as others he had filled her head with, like when he'd told her that a beetle caught by a swift over the French mountains might still be alive over the African desert, wriggling in its throat. Sophie hoped no one had seen her father spitting.

On the rooftop in Manhattan, Sophie looks again at her father's text. "How do swifts connect starlight with chocolate milk?" It is the only contact he has made since she walked out of the gallery yesterday without going to find him. The text refers to an old joke, one which, like most that have endured, he started. This one, of course, from the 'swift period', all those years ago, when Sophie's father started to believe "everything leads back to swifts." He used to sit in the garden, his eyes following their careering flight. They had returned from Africa, he said. As a child, Sophie pictured luggage tags the colour of brown sugar and duty-free Toblerone, but her father told her that the swifts had not touched a thing but insects and warm air in years. Sophie decided she would do the same, touch nothing but food and air, but this quickly proved challenging when she was reprimanded for trying to eat her lunch straight off the table. No one saw her throwing peanuts in the air later that day, pretending they were insects and trying to catch them in her mouth as a swift. No one knew that she tried as a teenager to sleep with her arms behind her back like wings.

From a young age, Sophie watched for the swifts too. She watched her father's face watching the swifts, and each year hoped as much as he did that they would arrive, because she hated seeing him lying on the bedroom floor when they didn't come. She mapped out the birds' migration paths on paper, a huge yellow blob for Africa, a tiny green one for England. She learned that despite weighing less than a peach or a teacup, swifts fly the equivalent of the distance to the moon and back seven times during their lifetime. They never roost there.

When the swifts did come, her father couldn't stand it when they left. He went to France and Berlin and Tel Aviv and West Africa.

Three days after her thirty-fifth birthday, Sophie went to New York. She walked The High Line, queued for bad-tempered gospel choirs, ate grits and waffles, walked streets named after letters of the alphabet.

She tried the city's poetry on her tongue, words instead of insects – "milk bar", "iced coffee", "apartment", "plantain", "lightning bug", "store" – in an attempt to disown "shop", "glow worm", "cafe", "flat", and "builders' tea", but she found herself dreaming of birds, drawing birds, and waking herself at dawn to hear their voices. She has become obsessed with the lock-up in the yard next door to Alice's apartment, which, two days after she arrived, she saw a woman unlocking to reveal twenty or so different caged birds that began to sing with the appearance of the light; sometimes finds herself at the window, hoping for another glimpse of them.

On the rooftop in Manhattan, Sophie imagines telling someone the story of sleeping naked on a roof in New York City. She will say that she felt closer to the moon. She stares up at the water tower above them, thinks about them squatting on rooftops all over the city, space ships made by children, imagining the weightlessness of launch. She deletes her father's text. She walks over to where her butterfly costume lies in a soft heap on the floor a few metres away from where the boy from Queens is asleep. On the way home tonight they got a cab from the subway. They'd been drinking Old Fashioneds. The boy from Queens told the driver that Sophie was his mistress and laughed. Sophie looked out of the window. He said she tamed songbirds for a living and put them in cages, allowing them only a brief glimpse each day of the sun. Sophie turned to see the driver looking at her in his mirror, and then away again. Now, she looks at the boy from Queens asleep for a brief moment, wonders who he actually is. She picks up the silken costume, tosses it over the edge of the building and walks towards the hatch without her clothes. The elevator doors breathe out, breathe in, swallow her, and spit her out on the ground floor, where she walks past the night clerk at his desk and out into the city's heat. There are lightning bugs flaming the grass in the park. She sits there until dawn.

S.P. Hannaway

S.P. Hannaway is drawn to the weird and wonderful. His first story appeared in Litro Online in 2014. Since then, his work has cropped up in journals such as *Dream Catcher, Brittle Star, Lighthouse, Neon, The Interpreter's House, Ambit* and *Stand*. He has recently completed an MA in Creative Writing at Goldsmiths. He has worked as an actor (in a previous life) and lives in London.

Love, Hunger

H alf light, half not. A numbing wind unsettles the gate.
His sheep: behind bars.
Jib's hand trembles. He grips the letter, crumples it.
Ready – is he? He stands, steels himself to deliver his
latest bumbling attempt, blunder.
  – Ears in gear, ewe? he stutters.

The ~~Shed~~

~~Hen,~~
~~Oh, Dear,~~
~~To,~~
You,

How to begin? To end?
  In his shed, his pen had jumped, misstep, misstep, stumbled down
the unlined paper. He tussled with the writing. His heart undid it.

Hen Woman of the purse strings, the house
I'm OUT

~~don't call me~~

Ninny
Ragwort Willy

untether

me

Jib teeters by the aluminium gate. A scarecrow of a man; his spare shoulders bunch up under straw-like locks of hair. His baggy blue cap is innocently cocked.

Rattled, he looks behind. Peers up at the louring farmhouse. Is there a watchy pair of eyes? Upstairs? Hen's? A sentry light burns in their once bedroom.

Turning back, he plays conspirator.

– What do *you* think, Hen?

His ewe is engrossed in chewing the cud. On the field-bound side, langled; cross-leg-tied so she can't stray, she seems to be contemplating his bony knees. Or: plotting an escape. He calls her Hen too – a name to spite his Mrs. The threadbare sheep is his confidante, his counsel. On bleaker days, he softly bends her ear.

– I've done your letter to me, Hen, when... you've had enough... of life. Now, lugs alert!

craaag
the height

Baaad maaan,

Jib titters, *baaas*; chuffed with his sheeply self.

Loner maaan of the Hunger field
I'm OUT
Oats or Feed or Graaass
NOW

untaaaangle

me

Glassy-eyed, he rehearses delivering the letter to his Mrs. He pops it through the gate bars – the field's unofficial letterbox – for a sniff of approval. But the sheep foot-stamps the thin-crusted earth, turns her skinny rump to him; snatches blindly at a low-lying blade of grass.

*

– Go on!
Clutching his tin, Jib shoos himself away as the early dark descends. A rake-of-a-man-on-the-run, unhitched, he flits across the hunger field, the clamped-down earth.
Empty.
All he's had to eat are bacon scraps. A plate is left on the step by the locked front door, for an animal, wanting.
Enough. Out.
Under the brooding presence of the house, he scrambles, through the concrete yard as shadows circle, dog him.
– Do it, Jib! Post it!

Woman of... the house

He daren't. Their old house creaks. It towers over him. Hen is likely inside, somewhere, upstairs, at her doll business – frantic manufacture, stitching madness. While Jib, he's barred, grounded; and in between them, pebbledash stone walls.

And vans: his and hers.

Dirt-spattered, hers, it guards the porch. Its dumpy unbudgeable backside is stuck in Jib's face. Hen drags off her homemade little 'uns in it on market days.

Hers blocks his. His out-of-work postie van is cornered. Hen is chief pilferer of keys.

As he blusters by the door he hears the letterbox, a slow scrape of weathered hinge, Hen's rasp.

– Evening, Weed!

It's one from a sackful of names for him, a sprouter of the field.

– Snake! he spits back, one from his own store.

Her peck sends him stomping down the rutted hawthorn lane. In the pocket of his thinning cords, letters weigh on him, the ink; the brunt of words, undelivered, unaired. He trudges into town with tin scoop in grubby hand.

*

Pure Feed is shuttering up shop. But he slips in. Someone has to get their oats.

Baaad maaan

Inside: a home away. Mineral scents run riot in his nose. Shelves of nourishment stack high. Fibre, pellets, coarse mix bags; unwind. It's where Bel works, his scarecrow woman. Likely, she'll tend to him. Has done before. She's behind the stubby counter, now, out of reach. Jib longs for reacquaintance.

– Anything you'd like? she asks.

He clocks her – sideways. Remembers her far-off eyes, painted lashes, thinly shape. He's always called her Doll: but not to her face.

If she was a proper doll, he'd deliver her to his potting shed in the hollow. He'd cherish her. Keep her in a box with a see-through window.

*

He comes from haggard land – his roots. Jib can't just unshackle. Stones tie his feet.

His father's field, Jib Senior, he left it. He made Jib promise, when he was Junior, to make something of it.

– *Flatten it.*

– *But Dada... the earth curves.*

– *Haul up the rock.*

– *But... it's crust, the best bit... loaf underneath.*

– *Blast the weeds.*

The ragwort comes, still, dots the hilly ground. Yellow-headed mountain soldiers advance.

He can't coax a single crop to grow. Hen, the breadwinner, and money-grubber, claims he's a meagre man of sticks, bone – no seed.

He doesn't get his oats.

Instead, 2, 3, summers ago, she brought back the yearling ewe from market, all grins, advising him *she'd* bring him warmth, *she'd* be company in the crooked field. Hen leaned in.

– Maybe you can have a little lamb?

He turned deepest beetroot.

– You... deliver.

Mornings, ingrained in him, he jumps into his radish-red van.

– Ninny!

The front door letterbox has a word.

– Wort!

It calls, names him.

– Willy! Rag!

There's little to write home about in his shed – a greasy dinner plate, a mound of paper awaiting words, his blue cotton cap snagging on rafter nails, and ragged boots trailing, as he travels its length.

1

2

3

There's foot room, a catwalk, alongside a mattress-for-one.

4

5

6

Baby steps allow an about-turn.

And

6

His headwear, he figured, would give him thinking room. Hen-fashioned, it was an old carry-bag for a doll. Now, sported upside-down, the handy drawstring binds it in place.

Baaad

5

Normally, he stuffs his wispy hair inside.

4

When the wind blasts his brains, his fool's cap points north.

Maaad

Hen: she's out there. Her wavering cry calls him to the field.

When he finds her, she's lying in the dirt, in a corner, at the mercy of the crows.

A fence divides the land with sagging barbed wire, posts driven cack-handedly. Thick thorn hedge runs in between, with privet and holly intermixed. But it doesn't keep a hunger-happy band of crows out, locals. At supper time – 5, 6 – they drop in. They dawdle. Something about this sheep smells underfed, tags her weak.

Theirs is a waiting game.

And Jib, scarecrow-man, watches Hen struggle; stand. It's a greeting. Blood dribbles down a left hind leg from the jutting hock. The black-beaks have staged their assault from the rear.

Jib launches himself into them, cap swinging. Disassembling, they retreat in a flap to the bare ash, nodding on the hill. He grabs Hen; forearm under rump, free hand grips the rope of the langle. He hoists her in his arms. She wrestles, headbutts, kicks. Hooves dig into ribcage. The sheep cries out against it. But he cradles her in the dip of the field. And there's warmth between.

– Hush! he whispers, nuzzling her.

He counts down the time

3

till dark

2

till sleep – the shed.

*

16
Acacia Lane
Flat b
No name scribbled inside the clear panel – Doll – but Jib knows she's above.

On Saturdays, there's piddling market traffic in the town – an odd stray van. He reruns the route even though he's unemployed now, let-go. All those undelivered letters. Slipshod, he was. His van, he dumps under the bare-branched acacia tree at the low end where, in summer, yellow flowers loll.

The satchel strap chafes his neck – missing letters, bundled brown, banded red. And an addition: a surprise, his – ~~mistake~~ – with no stamp.

Hawthorn Lane

Dear,
~~*Oh, Doll,*~~
~~*Er*~~
Bel,

His finger trembles as he buzzes.

I
You
The time... is always,

A shadow darkens the frosted glass panels. The door unlatches, opens only partly. Bel stands in the gap, flickers thinly, awkwardly. Slightly bewildered. Her bony hand reaches toward Jib. He gropes for words written, inside.

you,
do you remember back
2
3
summers

He separates the post, fumbles a from b, from c... but doesn't deliver. Time, he stalls it.

~~naked~~ days
warm
acacia days

His boots jig on the chipped diamond tiles. She eyeballs him.

in the boat, you on me, the river... loose

– Do you have something for me? she murmurs.

He hands over a sheaf of post, coarse-browns; probably bills.

~~Love,~~

Disappearing, she closes the door on him.

Jib

He fishes for his crumpled letter. Hovers next to the letterbox, trembling; slides it in.

*

Inside, in the little kitchen, adjacent, Doll, she's out of reach, and Jib, he perches at the narrow table with nothing, a single knife and fork, invited round – for supper, it said, her letter – and sounds drift through, glass, metal, the *clink-clink*, tinkering with a pot, stirring, the *plump-plump* of a stew, and he doesn't know where, how, to put himself, his hands, and his fingers dangle like straggling roots, exposed to air and dried out; too long spent shifting clods of earth, with stones for company, clasping to a hobbled sheep, Hen.

How does intercourse happen, again? A rekindling? When? Words don't work. If he had a pen, maybe...

it is always, now

...and, so, he takes to smoothing out the stark-brown linen tablecloth as if it was upturned earth, levels the folds, tries to flatten bumps, because he's starving, he, Jib, needs oats.

– Did I tell you, before... I like you? a voice trails through, tinkering still.

Bel appears, framed in the doorway, unblinking, doll-like. She's chopped her hair. She's taken scissors to it in the kitchen. She's shorn. Her charcoal eyes are larger still, more wanting, unreadable, and her arms wirier, more knotted. Her clothes hang stiffly. She brings odd glasses, a half-bottle of leftover red, a little dark-crusted bread. She eases next to him on the child-like bench.

In the carriage-clock quiet, sheeply warmth lingers between their bodies. Delicately, he lays a stick-like arm across her shoulders and there's a fit, almost. Her eyes wander; leave him. They travel places Jib can't. He prays he doesn't stink of Hen.

– There is no meat, she remarks, taking in the table, for herself.

For Jib, it's another hunger field.

*

In no time he's back, tripping up Acacia Lane. Can't afford to be spotted, a letter-less ex-postie on an unofficial round.

8

10

For you: nothing.

12

He fled his field before the weakly sun propped itself on an elbow, before Hen's van departed. And now, standing on the pavement in front of 16, on a fool's errand, he can't help himself.

Traffic behind, revs: the odd van heading for market square. One slows on the slope, flips gears, rage-riven, at his back. Hen? No, no. Is it?

He has a hall key from Doll – she doesn't like him loitering outside. Neighbours could see. Blinds stir: watchy eyes. So he clambers up the narrow winding stairs inside to the first floor, Flat b. Her doormat is awash – buff boats on a navy coir sea.

He knocks: timid.

Waits.

Nothing. For you: nothing.

– It's Jib!

He fishes out his thinking cap, clomps the length of the narrow landing.

1

2

3

his route, his out

4

5

6 feet of lankiness, he turns, slopes back to the door; drops on his knees. Eases open her letterbox, peers through.

– Doll?

He gulps. Doll – his name for her. She can't know he'd preserve her in a box. He blinks hard. His mouth opens to undo damage. Blinking, his vision blurs. Inside, there's a straw-haired boy, a little 'un, kitted out for the field. Could be a scarecrow child. It races down the furrow-thin hall, right-turns, topples, into the kitchen.

Clickety-click clack.

It could be him, a Jib, hidden, cooped up, unspoken of.

And his name?

– Junior? Jib whispers.

No sound.

– Willy?

Not a clack.

– Ninny? he toys, welling up.

– Rag?

Nothing.

– Hey, Yellow-top?

*

There's a gap between them – Bel   Jib – a thing unbridgeable. Their angled shoulders sit next to one another at the table. It's an emptiness; something heavy, a darkness like a midnight field.

Yellowy acacia light drifts in.

Half lit, half not, he tries to read her. Is there a letter inside, unwritten? There's a lack in him of words to entice hers out. He tries to put his arm around her, regain territory. She shrinks. There's something stuffed about her now, something concealed.

– Doll?

She doesn't blink. Now, she owns the name.

He would pour her wine, loosen time, but there are only dregs. Nothing. Hunger sits.

They could consume the letter placed between them on the table – the same paper as Jib's, same grain.

Bel's clung to his measly words?

it is always, now

It's time. It's now. He'll ask her if the clickety child is his. It's time to abandon Hen. He's penned the words. Though, they need fixing.

– This came, Bel says.

Out of nowhere, she produces a straw-haired, watchy-eyed doll in a carry-bag, drawstring gripping its neck. Props it against the bottle. Its mouth, stitched – a row of Xs. Seizing the letter, Bel's fingertips trace along the folds.

Jib's stomach drops.

– From Hen, love.

In his bones: the chill of rocky ground.

– Watch out, it says, for the scarecrow at your shoulder. Call him

Ninny, Willy Wort, Yellow-head. A hawthorn stick, he doesn't hold proper seed. He's empty.

Jib stares at the hunger table. Bel too.

– I need... a provider.

He isn't that. He thinks of his sheep, langled, starved. She can't escape.

*

Hen pokes her greyish snout through the gate to sniff Jib. His knees might be worth a nibble?

– No more oats! he scolds.

He reaches a hand through the bars to pet his confidante but she startles, backs off, ears like little flightless wings in the dimming light.

All the nights he's held her aloft... and skittish now, she doesn't know him. He's a stranger, a ...

Baaad maaan

He pulls out Bel's letter from his pocket, smooths it flat. There's writing on both sides, Bel's words scattered on the back of Hen's letter to her. He must have jumbled the two. Got the wrong end of the stick.

– You listening, Hen?

Yellow marbled eyes glare at him – a look that threatens I'll hunger strike if you don't feed me soon, I will! Wool-brained, she is. She foot-stamps in the bare field, the gloom. Ears flip forward, expectant.

You you...

– You get this, ewe?

The opening is sharp – frank, not Jib. She addresses him in a way that doesn't need a name. Though she dumped the letter in her letterbox for him to discover, unfold. Though she wouldn't open the door when he knocked, banged, rattled it, his coarse palms flat, scraping on the varnish.

Jangled, he peered inside the box flat; saw her, his Doll, stiffly propped at hunger's table, her back turned, unreadable.

His eyes glaze now, dart, as he skims; missing bits, gets muddled, desperate, mumbles life into words.

Acacia Lane

...you

        Yellow-head

...Wort

     Ninny...

Willy-rag

        a name, just a name, it ties you...

down

feeds you ... you are hunger

...empty

Jib

no

father...

        no...

        love,

He folds the letter. The words, they eat him, consume him. The wind sounds, unsettles. His sheep nudges the gate. Wants foddering.

On the height in the field Jib stands cradling Hen. His frame bows. It aches. He can make out his shed in the hollow, a blackened smudge of knocked-together wood. His bolthole, it's been padlocked – Hen's manoeuvre.

It is agony, the night.

The hours. His arms go numb. They sleep. When he shifts, Hen wakes; fettered still, fights to escape him, an unstoppable urge to find solid ground. Her ribs are like his fingers grasping, one with them. Lungs separate out. Muscled neck strains against him. She pants, trembling, hoarsely, cries upward.

Hunger. The hunger.

And cold, it swoops in. Inveigles its way into the two stomach rumblers. Freeze funnels through Jib's ears. Straw-man locks aren't enough to keep his noggin warm. But his blue bonehead's cap helps him think. Strange shepherd, in his mind, he pens a last letter to his sheep love.

it is always, now

Time startles. Skitters free. In early yellow-hued light, he hears the low moan of the animal-lorry, its approach. It navigates the lane. Its chassis scrapes on pebbled spine.

He daren't budge.

It charges up to his delivery gate, swings round – on the first pickup. Impatience etches the driver's face. He hears the ramp lower, the thud. Bel knows a man who knows the man. So, she'll get a cut.

Food: for Doll.

Spite: for Hen.

Jib turns. Ready – is he? He transports his ewe across the rocky ground. No heavier than a child. No growth.

On the blood-smeared ramp, Hen panics – flightless. Something hits her: the fear.

– Settle! he whispers, grappling, legs stumbling on the slats. – It's nearly over.

Ramp gates swing closed. She's fenced in. Again. But this time there's straw, a bucket: oats to distract her. It consumes her.

Jib lets go.

The dead-weight door swings up, haltingly, to enclose her.

Hen stares blindly, out.

Frances Hurd

Dr Frances Hurd has a longstanding interest in the social and emotional impacts of war which informs her fiction and nonfiction work. She has a PhD in Early Modern History and a professional background in education and heritage. Frances regularly writes and lectures on social and historical topics, and is currently exploring the period 1840 to 1940 through the lives of ten families linked by a single photograph.

Jackie and Pad

Da and Ma and me come here in 1900 when I was four-year-old, and I've been here ever since, save for the war. Da'd been an assistant agent on an estate in Donegal. Jack's father, Mr Buchanan, he stayed there a weekend and by the end of it he'd offered Da the job here at Courtland. He was thinking it would be good to have a man from outside Wexford to manage the place. He'd have no favourites, see? The Buchanans had had to let half the place go even then, what with so many saying feck this scraping a living from peat and stones, I'll try my luck in America. And they'd gone, walked off leaving their houses to fall into ruin and the fields to go back to the wild. Da was brought in to make it just a dairy farm, sell off what wasn't needed to the tenants. Mr Buchanan didn't want to be like his fathers before him, depending on the rents.

There was only us two young ones living on the estate. Jack was like my big brother almost, we was Jackie and Pad from the moment we met. If there'd been other children up here maybe it would've been another story, what boy wants a baby hanging at his heels? But he did, Jackie did. There was never a moment when I didn't know he thought I was the best company in the world. Our fathers was glad of it then, us two boys being such good friends.

I thought he was all the heroes wrapped into one, Cuchulain and all the rest of 'em. Jackie could ride any horse he put his leg across, he could make you fall down laughing, he could do anything he had a mind to. He was his father's only child, so Mr Buchanan wouldn't send him away to school. His two old uncles used to go on, saying Jackie was running wild, but Mr Buchanan'd just say this was his land, these were his people, and Jackie was in the best place he could be for the life he was going to lead.

Then when I was fourteen, Jackie was nineteen, we was up in the woods. There's a lot of trees been felled since, but then you could walk and walk and not see a soul most of the time. We sat down and he asked, he said, he asked if he could kiss me. He was my big brother or as good as, so I turned and put my arms round his neck, kissed him square on the lips. Well! That put the match to the fire and we went from there, once we'd started we couldn't get enough of each other. I couldn't see it was wrong but Jackie told me never to breathe a word to a living soul, and of course whatever he said was gospel.

Nearly two years we was lucky, and then his father's gamekeeper caught us at it. Beat me across the back with the butt of his gun, kicked me in the ribs and balls. He couldn't touch Jackie, not his master's son, but Jackie hit him, knocked him down. I was scrambling to get my clothes on, all over blood and bruises. We didn't say much. We knew we'd got to go to our homes and take what was coming.

My father beat me for the first time in my life, couldn't stand up the next day. When I come downstairs the day after, Jackie'd been sent to England, to the family of one of them old uncles. Jackie come back six months later a married man. I kept my head down, never stirred off the farm for over a year. Even so that fecking gamekeeper come after me with his little pals, come right in here to the yard. Da put a shot or three out the window and I set the dogs on to chase 'em.

I'll say one thing, we never lost money over it. Shops went on selling our milk and meat. It was good stuff, and they felt sorry for Da. When I went out doing deliveries there was plenty of remarks passed, though. Wasn't a soul round here didn't think I'd led Jackie astray. Da made me go to confession, half the town was hanging around to see me go in. All this time Jackie – Jack – and I never so much as looked at each other, though I knew, I *knew* he was cut to the heart same as I was. We'd never spent a day apart in all our lives up to then. Now if he come past Da touched his cap, which he never would've done before, and made me do it too. First time he saw that Jack went white. Kicked his heels in his horse and went straight off without a word. Two years like that. Two years.

His father died 1913, so Jack got the death duties and all to sort out, had to sell off almost all the land that was left. He and Mrs Jack, they'd had George by then, year old he must've been. Then the war came. Your man Redmond, he was a politician – you heard of him, maybe? – he was on about the Germans invading Belgium, and how Ireland was a little country too, it was the right thing to fight 'em.

I was in our barn and I heard Jack's step outside, I'd've known it in a thousand. 'We're joining up,' he said. 'You'll be my servant all through, Pad, I promise.'

'They won't take you,' I said. Strange, it was just as easy talking to him as though we'd been speaking every day. 'You're a married man'.

He shook his head, and he was smiling, he was my Jackie again. 'We're Irish,' he said. 'We make our own damned rules. They won't dare conscript us, so those of us who want to go, we'll do it how we want.' And he put his hand on my arm. 'I want you with me, Pad. I want to be with you.' I said I'd follow him to hell if he asked me to. Jesus, and we laughed about it!

It wasn't as easy as he'd thought for us to be together, but he managed it in the end. The two of us went off to fight – and others, but I'm the only one still living round here. Jack'd said to me I'd be his batman, and he got his way. I never laid a hand on him, nor him on me. I called him 'sir' and he called me 'Maloney'. But I woke him every morning, I kept his kit for him, I cared for his horse. And every now and then we'd have a few moments together on our own and we'd just look at each other and smile. Everything back here was all a long way away.

Then we was at Loos, October 1915 that'd be. I was waiting in line and he come past to take his place leading us over. He glanced at me and he was gone. And then afterwards I asked and asked, where was my officer? He'd been gassed by our own side and got invalided out. I was in France till the end. Nothing ever touched me save a bullet cut my cheek open, and another time I got a bit of shrapnel in my arse. No chance of getting home on leave, it's too far from France.

I just thought, it's good Jackie's safe out of it. I didn't know he was a fecking wreck, did I? He never said in his letters. Yes, we wrote. I wrote 'Dear Sir' and signed it 'yours respectfully'. Just told him bits about the battalion, anything funny I could think of, never anything anyone couldn't read. And he wrote about what he and my father were up to with the estate. He wrote 'Dear Maloney', but he signed it 'Yours ever'. I used to keep his letters tucked in my tunic. Used to put my hand up and touch where they were for luck.

Mother of God, what a shock it was coming back here. He'd been a big strong fella, Jack, and now he was a walking corpse, coughing and coughing. The gas'd eaten his lungs away. When I first set eyes on him I couldn't speak, just stood and stared with my hat in my hand. Then I saw he was crying. He took my hand and said 'I love you, Pad.' And God help me, all I said was 'I love you too, sir.' I hadn't called him

Jackie in so long, you see. Anyhow, I promised I wouldn't leave him again. Da had been dead three months from the influenza and Mrs Jack had gone off back to England with the baby, so there was just the two of us up here. He'd only got the big house left by then, and this, the Manor Farm, he'd made over to my father, so now it was mine.

I got him in his car and brought him over here, set him up a bed in the front parlour. I was past caring what anyone thought, for there was the stamp of death upon his face. So there I was working every hour God sent trying to run the place, and in between I'd be cooking, cleaning, doing anything he needed. Jack used to sit in a chair by the window whiles he was still strong enough, watching me going to and fro across the yard. There was a thick brown cardigan with a sheepskin collar he'd worn in the trenches, and I made him wear it all the time.

I woke up one night with him coughing, and the air thick with smoke. We could see out the window, Courtland was on fire. There was big houses going on fire then all over Ireland and neither the gardai nor anyone else cared a damn. We could see figures moving to and fro, they was looting the place. 'Ah well,' Jack said, 'so that's the end of that.' I closed the window and we went back to sleep. That was how much we cared about anything except each other.

My darling boy was wasting away like a little old man. Nights he slept propped up with pillows and my arms around him. In the end he slept nearly all the time with the morphine to help him, and who could grudge him that? Whenever he woke he'd start saying I mustn't leave him, and I'd tell him over and over, no, no, never again, my darling, my Jackie. And he'd say he loved me and drop back to sleep again.

Then he died. He died.

Fecking eejit I was, being surprised. Seen enough dead men before, why'd this one be any different? But it was, it was. My Jackie was gone.

He's buried down in the town. His cousins come over from England and put him in the vault under St Hugh's with the rest of the Buchanans. They told me not to come to the funeral and I told 'em don't worry, I won't. While they was tucking his body away in a great lead-lined coffin, I was up in the woods with the living trees. If he's anywhere now, that's where he'll be. I go up there and talk to him, and sometimes I hear him answer back. This is his cardigan I'm wearing, see? I pretend that it's his arms around me, though the smell of him's almost fled from it now.

So. There's the cows, and you've got to feed 'em, milk 'em, clean 'em out. Won't stop till the last of 'em dies or I sell 'em off. One day soon there'll be none left. That night I'll leave my cash box on the table and the front door wide open, and then I'll walk up to the woods. There's a place we used to go, quiet and hidden. If we'd've been in it that day that bastard wouldn't've found us. If I stay there long enough I know Jackie'll come and find me, young and beautiful on his grey horse. 'Jump up behind me, Pad!' he'll say, and off we'll go. After a few months there'll be maybe a few bones and a rag or two, and after a year there'll be nothing, nothing left of us at all.

Kate Lockwood Jefford

Kate Lockwood Jefford grew up in Cardiff, obsessed with books and cartwheels. She worked in the NHS and student mental health services – alongside a stint writing and performing stand-up comedy – before completing an MA in Creative Writing at Birkbeck, University of London. She won the 2020 VS Pritchett Prize and the 2021 Bath Short Story Award. Her work appears in *Prospect* magazine, MIR online, Brick Lane Bookshop Longlist (3rd prize 2020) and is forthcoming in Fish Publishing & Rhys Davies Award anthologies (2021) and *100 Voices* (Unbound, 2022). She's working on her first collection of stories, supported by a grant from Arts Council England.

Because We Are Weak

When I was a child, my mother used to say, *Sticks and stones.*

She used to say, *Actions speak louder than words.*

She used to say, *I'll punch you into the middle of next week.*

I imagined flying from her fist in an arc up and over the weekend to land on Wednesday.

All our mental processes – cognitions, wishes, desires, memories, unconscious phantasies etc. – are originally rooted in the body.

All around where we live, the criss-crossed metal arms of cranes – in red and yellow and blue – reach into the sky, piercing clouds, poised to swing and dip, to hook and hoist the bones and body-parts of new-builds. Hard-hatted men in high-viz vests swarm like Day-Glo beetles over scaffolding erected to flesh out the skeletons of these soaring towers.

I press my face against the window to watch the whole rackety shebang. The encroaching glass and concrete. Blotting out our slab of sky piece by pale-blue piece.

We go on holidays in search of skies touched only by church spires and mountain peaks. Sky to look up at, to dive into and swim.

We bring back souvenirs and dot them about the apartment.

A memory of the south of France. The seafront in Nice. After a meal in a restaurant, we ordered two more glasses of ruby-coloured wine. The proprietor brought the bottle over and poured. Glug, glug, glug. He left the bottle on the table.

Because we are weak, he said.

We sat watching a girl playing football with a boy on the promenade. To and fro, keeping the ball in the air, flicking it off their toes, backwards off their heels, running it along their shins. They were both really good. But she was better.

We finished the bottle.

A French couple live one side of our thin walls. We hear them fighting.

Ce n'est pas la meme!

His bass voice – gorged with rage – punching our heads. Hers a persistent wordless whine, a mosquito trapped in my ear.

From the other side we hear fists coming down on tables. Doors slamming and bouncing in their frames. A tap-tap-tapping on the glass partition between their balcony and ours when one locks the other out. We let whichever one it is through our flat so they can hammer on their own front door.

> In the context of a secure attachment relationship, bodily actions are
>
> gradually incorporated into progressively more sophisticated psychic
>
> functions as the mind develops.

I met my husband in a pub. I liked the way he wore his tallness with a slight stoop. Took it for granted he would have the words for the same misgivings as my own.

The barman said, *Be careful with that young man.*

As I make my way around this city, routes are barred. Bollards bash my knees. Pigeons under bridges shit on my shoulders. Tube trains wait until I get to the platform and then – *PPPPP* – slide their doors shut, pause a moment before lurching off.

I wake early to the sound of a child crying.

There are no children in this building. They're not allowed.

The local paper reports a woman in her forties was found dead from significant injuries behind the private girls' school around the corner from us. The school fees are stated. Three famous former pupils named.

The woman had no connection to the school.

Police appeal for witnesses and information.

I want to tell them I know her.

A patient tells me he fought with his ex-wife about money. She footed all the bills blah blah – he does actually say *blah blah*. When she told him their marriage was over, he cut the legs off their bed, carved them into crude images of himself, and gave them to her.

A patient tells me that when his partner puts him down, he goes out. Seeks men to fight. Men at bus-stops, in bars. Men who look at him with *what are you looking at?* faces. Men who suck their teeth. Who want it. After fists and smacks and punches, he feels physically exhausted. And mentally relieved.

Human aggression – behaviour intended to harm, humiliate or constrain

– may be understood as a manifestation of insecure attachment: a

defensive smashing up of feelings of vulnerability and weakness

triggered by real or feared abandonment.

I no longer have enough listening left in me for patients. I let my deaf mind drift.

I know I should be doing something else.

When I get home, I fold myself into the dark space beneath the stairs with the coats.

Like I used to as a child, hiding from the violence lurking everywhere.

When my mother calls, her words slip-slide down the line. She says she wasn't expecting to be on her own at her age.

She means not with a man.

She fills this vacancy with the priest – hems his vestments, embroiders lacy-edged drapes for the altar. Doilies for the myriad vases she arranges flowers in.

The priest calls her *Sister*, takes her hands in his and squeezes them. The only time another person touches her.

We never were a physical family. Not with affection anyway.

It is important to distinguish aggression from violence. Other related

nouns such as anger, rage, destructiveness, sadism, cruelty and brutality

are also often poorly differentiated and defined.

I am standing with my coat on, staring at the back of my husband's head. The back of his head he keeps close-cut. No bald patch, hardly any grey, hair that glistens with gel, that I sometimes smooth with the palm of my hand. Only not now because I'm angry. Fuming. Steaming from my nostrils.

The back of my husband's head doesn't move, doesn't swivel to face me, to speak to me.

This is what he does.

Earlier, over dinner, I told him about the disappearing sky, the bollards and pigeons and tubes. The dead woman. Told him how I can't figure out if something has been scooped out of me, leaving me feeling empty. Or if this feeling has been shovelled into me.

And when I'd finished speaking, he said, *Shall I start loading the dishwasher?*

And I wanted to slice his useless ears off. My head flooded with ferocious words I lobbed like Molotovs.

You always. You never.

Then I stomped off and got my coat.

Now: the back of my husband's head.

Be careful with that young man.

His silence screams at me. I am on the verge of more words. Words I fear could crack us so badly we'd always see the join.

I go for a walk.

All behaviour may have an aggressive function, whether negative – e.g.,

withholding – or positive, symbolic, or carried out.

In the beginning, we didn't row. We knew the words but we didn't say them. I was afraid of breaking us. Him.

In the beginning, we lived on opposite sides of the river. He sent me postcards. Carefully selected words put together in sentences that throbbed with wit and charm.

He sent me flowers.

White lilies? my mother said. *Aren't they for weddings? Or is it funerals?*

My mother came to our wedding with her third husband, who cornered me to say she'd left divorce papers on their bed that morning.

The city smells of dust, dry air, petrol fumes and pigeon shit. I head in the opposite direction to where the dead woman lay, pausing to listen to the rushing of the river Fleet beneath a grating on the road outside a nearby pub, wishing it were running through me, cooling, rinsing out silted-up resentment.

The pub was once a hub for bear-baiting. A she-bear chained to a stake, claws and teeth removed, set upon by pit-bulls tearing chunks off her while she lunged helplessly, spinning on her chain, drooping, dribbling slime and blood. Bets were made. If she was down three minutes the dogs won.

One time a bear turned on the landlord and strangled him in clawless paws with her final grasp. I picture her gripping, squeezing, his airway collapsing, bear and man falling.

My path is heaving. Hordes of people down the street, across the bridge, along the river. People shoving shoulders, elbows and bags into me, spinning me round. Clawing, pawing. People behind screens. Stopping for selfies with St Paul's. Or the Tate, the Shard, the Globe.

I read about couples falling to their deaths taking selfies. The sea wall in Cascais. A ledge in Yosemite.

I wonder if these people didn't fall but were pushed.

My mother told me that when I was six months old, she'd found a receipt for a restaurant in my father's pocket. At first, she thought it was romantic: him keeping the receipt from the night he proposed. Until she saw the date. Same place, different woman.

She told me she considered strangling him with a ball of wool. Spearing an eye on a knitting needle. Crashing her sewing machine over his head.

In the end she used her hairbrush. Split his lip, chipped his teeth, blackened his eyes, broke his nose.

He was a boxer, she said. *People thought he must've done it in the ring.*

Violence is distinguished from aggression as actual bodily harm inflicted

by one person on another, in which the body boundary is breached and

physical injury caused.

My husband has never raised his voice to me, never spoken in rage or cruelty. If he did, he says, he'd feel like a monster.

He lets the monster live in me.

Be careful with that young man.

It's not true about sticks and stones. Words, once said, can't be unspoken. They hang in the air, echoing in our heads, bouncing off our bones.

Words hurt. But they don't wound or kill.

Ce n'est pas la même!

When he's hurt, my husband's eyes change from green to grey. I sense him take a step away from me, so he is no longer quite there, fully in his own skin.

It takes him at least a day to recover.

On one trip, we drove 350 miles in silence.

There's a gust in the wind which blows my skirt up. Exposes my knees. The knees I chose this skirt to hide. My mother's knees.

My husband says I'm nothing like my mother.

Or his ex-wife.

I pass a young woman who looks as if she's been unwrapped from a box tied with silk ribbon by a perfumed assistant in a high-end Paris store. Her face has the ceramic sheen of a Toby Jug. Serene. Is she the kind of woman my husband would prefer?

In my mind I lift and hurl her head-first to the ground, smashing her to bits.

I step into a bar for a drink. A stack of red paper napkins on the table. As I sip my wine, I tear one into strips. A pile on my table like entrails.

> Acts of bodily harm may be consciously or unconsciously motivated, but
>
> often hold symbolic meaning, although this meaning is usually not
>
> available to the mind of the violent person.

When I get home my husband is where I left him. I am facing the back of his head.

This is what he does.
The dishwasher swishes and churns.
I imagine it's coming from inside his head.

Our electric bulb-lit window is a mirror. Reflecting a man sitting at a table. A woman standing behind him. On the wall, a metal tray: a picture of a wide blue sky over the bay of Nice.
I need to know what is in his head. I need his words.
I hear a child crying, closer now. From somewhere deep inside me.

And I watch the woman   in the mirror act of her own volition   she twists her body reaches her right arm across her left shoulder   unhooks the tray   clasps its edges   and raises it   in both hands   above his head.
Be careful with that young man.

Vijay Khurana

Vijay Khurana is a fiction writer and translator from German. He won the 2021 Griffith Review Emerging Voices Competition, and his stories have been short or longlisted for numerous other prizes, including the Desperate Literature Prize, the Galley Beggar Press Short Story Prize, and the Cúirt New Writing Prize. His fiction is forthcoming in *NOON* (US) and *The Griffith Review* (Australia). Vijay has also been a presenter on Australian radio station triple j, and in 2014 he published a children's chapter book, Regal Beagle.

Follower

The valley was too perfect, too symmetrical. Its vertical sides sank in an unnatural arc, curving down to a flat expanse. The snow stopped in a jagged line on the rock, leaving a broad grey smear above the grass and the darker green of conifers. Below us, on one side, a waterfall appeared from nowhere and fell into a white river. I thought I could see flowers down there, a great carpet of purple and yellow, colours I hadn't seen in months.

We didn't have much except a tarpaulin and the camel-packs we had stolen. You were wearing a jacket you had taken off one of the girls. It was small but it looked warm. Your face was chafed from the cold, though unlike me you were old enough to have fine, brown hairs on your jaw and lip.

'Look there,' I said, as we passed beside a ridge's shadow, 'the last of the snow.' It felt important to do something, like a ritual, so we each made a snowball and threw them out of the shade, into the sun.

'The kind old sun,' you said. 'As we go down it will only get warmer.'

We didn't talk about the place we'd left, the freezing dawns, the monitors, the others. We'd been liberated. As we walked, you told me the story of two explorers who would have survived if they had done things differently. They were trying to find a way across a mountain range so the land on the other side could be turned into farms. The mistake they made was not sticking to the ridges. If they had stuck to the ridges, they would have made it, but they went down into a steep-sided valley and they never found their way out. I said they probably had no choice about it, that they probably needed water. They would have died on the ridges anyway, I said, of thirst. You agreed, and said it was a pointless story. We didn't have that problem. Our camel-packs were filled with melted snow; we sucked at them royally, whenever we felt like it, without breaking stride.

Soon came the first tree, a scrawny young conifer a little way above the others on the slope. We raced each other to it, you a couple of steps ahead, more confident on the incline. You had always been athletic. At the camp you'd sometimes wanted someone to spar with you after a meal, body-punches only, nothing above the chest or below the belly. The game was trying to make the other one vomit. I'd seen my share of losses, but fewer than some of the others. Plenty were afraid of you, but we were friends, as much as there had been friendships. I had come with you, after all.

You reached the tree well before me. When I caught up I grabbed at it, light-headed and panting; the thin trunk flexed in my hands and the needles bit my skin.

'That was a bad idea,' I said, and we laughed through our tight chests.

I sat down to rest and you put your hands on the tree to see how far you could bend it. It was as thick as a wrist, not even that. The needles didn't seem to bother you. You forced it into a teardrop shape before the fibres opened with a sharp snap.

We were heading for the river, a continuous descent that made my big toes ache where the toenails met the skin. Occasionally I could smell your body mixed in with the scent of pine; with each breath my stomach hurt a little more. I marvelled at the songs that came into my head, old songs from when I was young. For no reason at all, I started humming a saxophone line from a CD my father had once brought home. I was surprised when you hummed along with me. I'd never thought anyone outside my family would know it. But you knew things, you were always one of the sharpest. I'd heard a monitor say that all you needed was discipline and one day you could be a monitor too.

'That's a good tune to have stuck in our heads,' you said. 'It doesn't have a chorus so we won't drive each other crazy with it.'

Still, I hummed the saxophone line until you told me to stop. You were sensitive about repetition. At the camp, when we had gone around the circle reciting the same words to each other, I'd often watched you shaking your knee and chewing your cheek. When your own turn came, you'd make the pledge loudly and clearly, but with a dullness in your eyes.

We walked down a slope covered with shale, digging our heels in and leaning back, our steps playing melodies on the loose rocks. The waterfall was out of sight, but I could still hear a low, constant whisper. We stopped and took out the potatoes I had stolen, grating them against our teeth and holding the raw pap in our cheeks. There hadn't been time to take anything else. We took turns throwing discs of shale as far as we could, listening to them clatter or smash. My arm burned each time, but I liked the bright sounds they made. You picked up a couple of the thinner ones to take with us, saying we could grind the edges and use them as knives.

''Cause suicide is painless,' I sang suddenly. The potato in my mouth made it sound like my face was swollen. 'How did that get into my head?'

'*M*A*S*H*,' you said. 'You were thinking about potatoes, and that's the theme from the TV show.'

What a mind could do, all on its own, without a person even having to think. I hadn't heard the song in a long time, but it was all still there: my father's CD collection, the red and white spine that read SMALL SCREEN HITS, the remote control that made the volume knob on his stereo turn. Just then I had to fight the urge to say something childish, to ask if we were going home.

'If only we *could* mash them,' I said. 'With butter and herbs.'

You didn't say anything, and I thought about my father chopping herbs, the sound of a knife on the wooden board, the pot lid rattling as the water boiled. My mouth flooded with thick, sour saliva, and I spat.

We walked in silence, sucking the straws of our camel-packs. Whenever I stopped to pee, you would keep going and afterwards I'd have to jog to catch up. My pee was clear; watching it come out made my headache worse.

At lunchtime we reached the river, a shallow and determined rush of melted snow, showing us which way to go.

'Do you still have the string?' I asked.

You nodded, sucking juice from your potato.

'We should try to catch a fish,' I said.

You unzipped one of the jacket pockets and took out a red reel that looked like it should be attached to a kite. There was also a booklet with a plastic cover, the kind of souvenir people get stamped in different national parks to prove they've been there. There were no outside books allowed at the camp, so the girl must have kept it hidden. It must have meant something to her. You took the plastic off and bent the spine over, then dug out one of the staples. It shone silver in your palm and you said, 'We could turn this into a hook, maybe.'

You were sceptical about using potato as bait, but you went along with it. I bit off a tooth-sized nugget from mine.

We saw some fish, but they were tiny, far too small for the potato chunk. A couple of them came to nibble at it, though. You said it was a good idea, that we should try again downstream, where the fish would be bigger. I loved feeling useful around you.

"'Cause suicide is painless,' I sang, blissfully, but I didn't know the next line. I sang it again. You were silent as we walked. I made myself stop before I annoyed you and ended the good feeling between us.

We were following the edge of the river. Beside it was a foot-wide crease where nothing grew, but we couldn't tell if it was a proper path. There was a springy carpet of dead pine needles; the flowers I thought I'd seen weren't there. The sun was behind us now, inching into the mountains we had left behind. It had been more than a day since we'd eaten anything but potato. I was for stopping to try fishing again, but you said we should keep moving in case anyone had followed, that we would wait until the river was deeper and wider. You sounded confident, relaxed. I couldn't understand how your stomach didn't feel like mine did, knotted and aching.

'If we had a plastic bottle we could make a trap for the little ones,' I said. 'I've seen it done. You cut the top off and put it back on upside down, like a funnel. The fish swim in and can't get out again.'

'We don't have a bottle,' you said.

'If we did, we could cut it with one of your sharp rocks,' I said. 'There was no more shale around but you still had those two bits; I could hear them clicking in your pocket as we walked.

We tried sucking grass together with the potato. It was earthy, bitter. It made the pain in my stomach worse. I spat mine out, potato and all, and you said, 'Careful.'

As it started to get dark we found our strides were in synch. We looked at each other and laughed, pretending we were marching. Then you took my hand and we swung our fists back and forth. That felt nice, and I almost forgot the soreness in my head and stomach. Soon we would have fish, then we would get to a town and work out what to do next. We were a team.

We stopped to pitch the tarpaulin between two trees. I wanted to fish but we needed the string for the shelter and you said we should put it up before it got dark.

'It's not even raining,' I said.

'There'll be dew. It'll get cold.'

We lay down side by side. I put my hand into the elastic of my underwear and let my warm palm soothe my abdomen. Beyond the tarpaulin I could just see the outline of the valley's lip.

I was asleep in seconds, but I woke again after what seemed like only a few minutes. You were awake, wrapped in the small jacket, not doing anything, just watching the night.

At the camp we had slept in the same cabin, and we sometimes talked at night, when everything else was quiet. I wondered if that was still possible.

I said, 'We had to get out, didn't we?'

I could hear you chewing your cheek. Then you nodded and your chin made a swishing noise against the jacket.

'I had to get out,' you said.

'Me too,' I said.

When I woke up again it was light and I felt as if I'd been hit on the head. Your jacket was next to me but you were gone. I thought you might have gone to try fishing without me, then I realised the string was still holding up the tarpaulin. I thought about calling, but I knew you wouldn't like that. I went to a tree and peed. That hurt too. In the jacket I found the hook you'd made. I carefully took down the tarpaulin and put rocks on top so it wouldn't blow away.

The taste of my potato made me sick. The flesh was streaked with brown veins which hadn't been there the day before. I squatted, spitting what I'd tried to eat and retching a ribbon of orange bile. I stayed like that for a while, with my head in my hands, looking at the mess I'd made, then I dug out a piece of potato with my thumbnail and speared it on the hook. At the river was a large slab of rock. I lay down and looked at my reflection. We have to wash, too, I thought. I wanted to put my head in that cold water, all that melted snow; it would numb me. But first I was going to surprise you with a fish. There was a flash of movement in the reflected sky, and another. The fish were grey with black specks, not big, about the size of a finger. I let the string and hook fall into the water. I would have to wait. Blood was running into my head, but I was determined.

It was strange to be fishing. I remembered arriving at the camp, how they'd given us a sheet of paper printed with the words, *Follow me, and I will make you fishers of men.* Below was the line, *I will follow,* and a blank space for our names. Afterwards they'd laminated them and stuck them up by our beds. I guessed by now the monitors would have taken down yours and mine, and thrown them away.

I heard the tarpaulin crackle and imagined you watching me. Two fish had turned as though they had noticed the bait, but they didn't come close. I heard footsteps, the sound of you getting nearer until your shadow fell across my body.

'There are fish here,' I said. 'I just need to get one.' I heard a scrabble of rocks and you knelt beside me, putting a hand on my back to steady yourself as you leant over the edge.

'Keep very still,' you said, 'or they'll get scared.' I could see our faces swimming in the water.

'I can do it,' I said. 'Then we'll have breakfast. If we can make a fire we can cook them, otherwise sushi.' I tried to laugh, but your weight was pushing my chest into the rock.

Before we left the camp you had said nothing to me, except, 'Go and find some food.' There wasn't much to take. The good stuff, the flour and sugar, was locked in a metal chest, and that was too heavy to carry. The potatoes were on the ground by the rack. They'd probably fallen out of a bag. I saw the camel-packs and grabbed them. I figured you'd be happy I'd thought of water, but you just stared at the potatoes and told me we had to leave. Until that moment I hadn't imagined you'd take me with you. I sensed you had done something, but I didn't ask what. I didn't want to go into the cabin to see. But you were wearing someone's jacket, a girl's jacket, I could see that.

As I stared into the river I felt your body shift, a heavier weight on my back. The fish watched the bait, darted closer, formed an uncertain arc around it. Somehow they were able to stay completely stationary as the current flowed around them. Then one went even closer. It was an inch away.

'I promise I'll catch one for you,' I said. My voice came out like a whine. 'It'll be just for you. I can do it.'

'It just seems so unlikely,' you said, and shifted again. There was more pressure between my shoulders, more of you. It felt like you were kneeling on me. I tried to turn and look but you put a hand on my head to stop me. Your fingers were warm in my hair, tight against my skull. I wanted to say something, like 'Please,' but I didn't. I had followed you down here, into the valley. My head was thick with blood, and when I tried to close my eyes I found I couldn't. The water was so clear. It was magnifying the fish. I could see them better now. They weren't grey at all, but a yellowy green, and their black eyes had orange rings around them, and their tiny mouths were open. I longed then for the icy touch that would come when I broke the surface. You pushed me closer, until my head had gone as far as my neck would allow. The fish scattered.

Blaine Newton

Blaine Newton is an award-winning playwright with an audience of well under a million people. When not bragging about himself in the third person, he has written monologues for radio shows you've never heard and short stories for magazines you've never read. Blaine lives in Edmonton, Alberta, Canada, far enough north that on occasion the crackling of the aurora borealis will wake him from his writing-induced stupor.

Life in a Bottle

The ground was soft for digging and the sky was dark – no moon, but an occasional sweep of light from the traffic on the road high up at the top of the embankment.

That was the summer of the heavy rain. The rains that caused the spruce trees to explode with green pine cones that littered the ground like goose shit – the cones that smelled so good crushed in your hand – tossed in the boiled water – their sharp taste keeping the hunger away a little longer.

Maybe it wasn't so bad as that. Beth handled it best. Every few weeks or so she'd take us to the University, where the research people would buy a pint of our blood. Cash – not much, but enough that pooled we could get a jug or two of beer in the campus pub. Being down a pint would make the buzz come faster and stay longer. But there were forms to sign – I don't like to make my name – give my name – to them – to anyone.

Even Beth didn't know my name – or if she did, she didn't use it. Love, she called me – "Luv" it came out as, in her English accent – her soft accent – consonants littered or lost – like all the edges had worn away. And I didn't know anything about her – except her first name. I didn't ask. Two years we were together. I never asked. Or if she told me, I've forgotten. I've forgotten so many things, I think.

On the street it wasn't easy anymore to put the touch on someone. It was different when I was younger – before they changed the rules. You can't ask for money now. Now you can't touch anyone – can't even look them in the eye. Too aggressive, they say.

Before I'd just come up to some guy on the corner as he waited for the light to change. No escape. I'd come up – big, but friendly – drop my heavy hand on his shoulder – laugh loud – call him "buddy," like I know him – like I give a shit. And he'd throw some coins at me – to make me scramble – to get away. I'd just laugh – Yell "thanks, buddy!" – as cheerful as I could – at the retreating crowd he'd disappeared into – the crowd on my side of the street parting around me.

Now I'm too threatening. Not my size – people can deal with that. It's my face – the scars my few yellow teeth, like fangs – the way my head jerks – twitches when I'm angry or hungry or tired – or when I hoard my meds to sell on the street – or when I can't be bothered to check in at the clinic regular like they want me to.

People back away now – like they'll catch something – like I'm breathing something into the air that they'll carry home to their family – that'll turn their kids into me.

Not a problem for Beth. She has this smile – that waif look that gets sympathy – that makes people think of a distant daughter or sister who just needs a few dollars to make it right. Her clothes aren't new, but they're not torn or dirty. She's careful with them. Soft tones with a splash of colour like her voice – like a soft laugh. Most days she wears them high on the shoulder to cover the tattoos – hiding the swirls of artwork.

And she'll make our signs sometimes. They let you use signs – no speaking, but signs are okay. She'll find the cardboard flap from a box – take it into the library and borrow a marker and do the lettering. Not that I can't write – I can – but my hands are big and clumsy – my block letters look hard, like a shout. She has curves to her letters – adds a happy face or a butterfly – makes the message seem positive and real – draws the loose change from unsure hands – coins collecting in the empty Tim Hortons cup in front of us. The sign that says we're from out of town – we just need a few dollars to get back – to return home – leave the area – stop being a burden here – be someone else's problem.

And when we've been too long on one corner – when they recognize us – when they can no longer be part of our lie – she'll put the cardboard down on the sidewalk – salt it with a few coins – start singing softly – folk songs and lullabies from her home – from when she was young. Her high, pure tones sound so sweet that I'll rest my head against the brick and sleep – dreamless for a change – float on her song – wake to see our small stack of coins grown to something that'll get us through another day or two.

Before the snow comes, we sleep in the woods by the river – in the protected land – where the bank down to the water is too steep for houses – the ground too unstable to build anything lasting. We have a lean-to I made from fallen trees and a tarp I took from someone's back yard – that had protected their expensive car from sun or rain or hail. Orange. Bright, like a toy – all tied together with yellow plastic cord. I know how to tie knots – make it secure – keep the wind from carrying it off.

The lean-to's okay, when the weather's warm – or when Beth and I are close together under the blanket – or when we've scored something to take the chill off. And the sound of rain is nice – like fingers tapping – like a ticking clock in a hallway.

When the snow comes – when the frost hardens the ground – when the frost turns my hair white and we wake in the morning – my knees stiff so I walk like an old man – then we try to move inside. But the shelters are no good. They split us up in different rooms – make us sleep on mats on the floor – so close you can smell the next guy – makes your sleep fitful – your dreams overlap with theirs. People steal your stuff. No respect. Animals. You have to leave early in the morning. You can't be drunk or high.

So we find somewhere – a building left open – a back window I can break without too much noise – a stairwell. But now there are so many cameras and alarms, and we have to watch the time so we aren't caught. Get up early like a worker – gather our things and be gone before anyone sees us – move from spot to spot so we don't get too comfortable – get too lazy about it. Get caught and we get our asses kicked by the cops. Get angry – get angry and they kick you more.

I've worked. I've had jobs – when I was younger. I carried things, when I could. Stacked boxes in warehouses. Picked up trash. Painted fences and lamp poles. Was a soldier for a while. Or maybe I dreamed that was when I was a kid. But that's been painted over too.

I worked in a slaughterhouse when oil prices were high – when they'd take anyone. They gave me a bolt gun for "knocking" the cattle – pressing it to their forehead and fired a bolt. Sometimes they'd move at the last second and you'd miss – hit a vein – blood spirting out all over you – the sudden iron smell. The first cow of the day was okay, but once there's blood in the air – the other cows smell it – smell the fear – the kill floor stinks with the ammonia smell of piss. I lasted three days. Maybe it was the killing – or the need to be sober.

And I cooked. I liked doing that. Someone taught me so I'd have something to do when I got out – to keep me out – something for me. Now – over an open fire – using an old coffee can –I'll make Beth and me tea sweetened with the sugar and cream we take from the outdoor tables – can't go inside anymore. Or use the pine cones I've scooped from the ground and stuffed into my pockets. Stew, sometimes – or soup – if we have a little extra for a can of this or that.

People will give us stuff too – if they're not okay tossing coins in the hat – not okay us using the money how we want or need – not how they think it should. Sometimes people will toss sandwiches on our cardboard – the half they didn't want. Sometimes they're wrapped tight, like they brought it special from home – thought special of us when they made their own lunch that morning. Those are good.

One guy said he wouldn't give me money, but he'd take me to a place for soup or coffee – so he'd know how his money was spent.

I pushed him – when he tried to touch my arm – when he tried to lead me – take my arm like a child or an idiot. Pushed him into a wall – not hard – but too hard. I'm too big. He fell. Staggered up. People came – a half circle of them with me against the wall – the smear of blood on the brick. We had to go – Beth and me – find another corner to sit on – another wall to rest against.

Then came the night when we were sleeping in the woods. I woke on my back to the smell of something burning – like the woods were on fire – the stars above exploding like fireworks – the sky all quick short bursts. I tried to wake Beth for her to see, but my words were mumbled and when she finally woke, she stared at me. I tried to point to the sky. But my arm wouldn't move from my side.

Some of its use came back – slowly – but I push my right hand in my pocket now so it doesn't seem obvious. And my speech came back – mostly – enough that Beth can understand me. But some sounds I can't make. Some letters. My name. Now I mispronounce myself.

Sometimes Beth and me we eat at the soup kitchen – when it's cold or we're really hungry. Get the beef and potatoes and gravy and soft vegetables. I don't like the look of the servers, though the volunteers

– who give you an extra scoop of this or that and a sly wink like they make all the difference – like it's all about how good they are – to be volunteering – to be helping someone like me.

I hear them, as I move down the line – heads nodding in my direction – "look at him" – "poor fellow" – "if only" this or that – like they know my story – like they know who I am – like their measured scoops make a fuck of a difference to me. Like a second dessert will save me. Fatten me up for Jesus. Like I'm their sacrifice that'll get them closer to their god – buy their own salvation.

I take the food. I fill my stomach against the cold – against the hollow week. But afterwards – I'll go out to the parking lot – squat on a car – shit on a car – just to show them.

Beth doesn't like that – cries sometimes – says we need them. And I feel bad. But I don't think they notice – notice even that – cause next week they're back – still smiling – still the wink like they maybe know but they don't. Like I'm supposed to say something.

Sometimes I start to shake so bad the tray spills – the fork and knife hit the floor at my feet with a broken bell sound – and Beth has to take me to a table to sit down. And she'll stand there – hold me until the shaking stops and I can eat – stand behind me, her arms reaching up to drape over my big, useless frame. Or she'll sit on my knee – feed me – wipe the gravy from my chin with the thin paper napkin – scraping the pudding from the side of my mouth with a spoon as I clutch my elbows trying to keep everything from spilling out.

But the servers, they won't come over then. As I shake, they disappear. Suddenly there's something they need to do in the kitchen – out of sight.

I used to catch birds. Small birds. Sparrows. Chickadees. Cedar Waxwings. Beth knew all the names. Nothing cruel. I just noticed in the fall that they liked to eat the berries on a certain kind of tree – red berries that had passed ripe – started to ferment on the branch. They'd get drunk, these birds, and fly all crazy like – flop on the ground – too stoned to fly. So I'd pick those berries – all I could find – and place them on the ground. Hide back in the bushes or around the corner – protect the area from cats and the like – wait until the birds were good and drunk and then go and pick them up. Gentle. Put them in an old shoe box. Walk with my box of drunken birds to a guy I knew. I don't know what he did with them – pets maybe or pet food. Food for a snake. I only know I got 25 cents each.

Beth never liked it when I caught birds. She thought it was mean. So I told her the guy had a pet store – that he sold the birds to families – so the birds would live inside with food and water – protected from anything that would prey on them. I told her they would sing – teach children how to whistle. She liked that. That settled her – calmed her. I could do that – calm her. Talk to her. Maybe that was my purpose – between the shaking and the bullshit – my sudden anger. To give Beth someone to care for – someone worse off than she was.

And she would always keep one bird – pick it up from the ground – cradle it until the berries wore off and it could fly again.

Now the ground was soft again for digging, so I could make the sides of the hole smooth – the corners sharp – using the shovel we took from the City truck when the crew went around the corner for a smoke. I can do good work when I want to. I can take pride in what I do. At least I used to, I think.

I kept the hole shallow, though. No more than waist deep on me – although that's plenty deep on Beth. Anything deeper is a waste. Unnecessary. Stupid. A hold-over – from what and where and why I don't know and can't remember.

As I dug, Beth sat a few yards away, her back against a tree. The bird in her hands began to twitch – roll over – one wing waking up faster than the other – sporadic efforts that made it dance around on the platform she made of her open hands – palms upward – like an offering – level with her chin so she could watch over it – judge when it was ready.

Just as I was finishing – just as I drove the shovel into the pile of waste dirt at the top – the bird seemed to recover and flew to a perch several feet up. Beth stood. For a moment they were eye-level – she still, it twitching and darting. Finally, it was gone. She turned back. Me standing in the hole – we were eye-to-eye now, me and Beth.

"Time?" she asked – no expression in her voice, but tired, I thought.

I nodded. Lay down at the bottom of the hole. Full length. Restful. Crossed my arms over my chest.

"You never sleep like that," she said.

"You can rest the bottle under my hands. That will protect it. When you start shovelling the earth in. There aren't any rocks – but a clump might break it – break the bottle."

She shook her head – muttered something, looking at the shovel.

I'd gotten tired, that's all – can't take care of myself – shake all the time. I can't take care of Beth. I'm slow. Hurt all the time. Some days I can't stand straight. I'm a danger to her. She's taking care of me – it's a waste of her time – her energy. She could do better without me. I'm too big. I scare people away. She could always do better with a smile – without me in the shadows – arms crossed, rocking on my feet, trying to keep warm – never warm anymore, even in the summer – trying to keep away – in the shadows – trying not to be seen or to be obvious.

So I told her. Wrote this out so you'd know. If you found me.

You see, it's got to be clear – if I'm found – if I'm ever found – that nothing happened. Beth's not responsible. It was my idea.

I said for her to drive the shovel into my neck. I asked her. I showed her where. Scratched a line on my neck with my nail. Even took a rock and ran it over the edge of the shovel blade to sharpen it. But she knew it would take two, maybe three blows – knew that the first would be the hardest, but once I was hurt – once I was bleeding – twitching like one of her birds maybe – me bleeding out like I was smeared with berries. She knew her heart would tell her that she had to hit me again – and maybe again – that it would be kindest – that it would make my pain go away. Then she'd cover me up with the dirt – as I bled out – it was all how I asked her to do it. She's strong. Steady. Not like me.

It's what I wanted – to die like that – like – like a soldier – like a knight or something – something I thought I remembered from stories I read as a boy. Or saw in a play. Adventure stories. Heroes. Quests. Purpose.

But I looked at her – into her eyes – saw how wet they were – saw for maybe the first time in my big, stupid life what I did to someone else. That it would hurt her. So I reached into my pocket and took the pills – the medication I'd been hoarding over the months – the stuff they'd give me at the clinic – never thinking to ask why I was showing up regular for a change – after so long.

I took all the pills – washed them down – emptied the bottle – this bottle. Choked back the vomit – the fight.

She touched the handle of the shovel – walked past it – slid down into the hole. Knelt by me. She took the bottle from me – the empty bottle – promised to roll up this story – our story – write down the story I'm telling – place it inside. For if I'm ever found.

In my dreams, she puts the bottle under my hands. Pressed her hands against mine. Kneels next to me – looking down on me. Kisses my forehead.

Then rests her tiny head on my chest – like it was any other night – waits for me to calm – waits for me to sleep.

Ajay Patri

Ajay Patri is a lawyer by training and has worked in a law firm and a think-tank in the past. Earlier this year, he was selected by the South Asia Speaks Mentorship Program, as part of which he is working alongside Madhuri Vijay, the author of *The Far Field*, on his first novel. He lives with his wife in Bangalore, India.

A Need for Shelter

The man brought me to a flat in a decrepit building and told me I would be staying there. It's not exactly the middle of nowhere, he said, but it's as close as it gets. He waited for me to react to this, his eyes wide in anticipation, his mouth a little open. I didn't know what kind of reaction would be appropriate, so I turned my attention to the wall of the living room instead. I touched it and a flake of dried paint drifted to the floor.

If my lack of enthusiasm disappointed him, he didn't show it. Anyway, he continued, here's a list of things you can't do.

He handed me a piece of paper torn from a legal pad. As I perused the items on it, he stood beside me – so close that I could smell his minty aftershave – and read the points out loud as if I couldn't do it myself.

No loud noises, no major alterations, no parties, no boozing, no cooking stuff that's too pungent, no pets, no going off elsewhere without notifying us first. Pretty simple, eh?

I folded the paper in half and kept it on the table. The table and the chair beside it were the only pieces of furniture in the living room. The bedroom, which I could see through its open door, had a mattress on the floor and two bedsheets. The man took a step back and all I could smell again was the faint odour of mould growing in the corners.

It's not much, he said, but it's home, isn't it?

*

The street outside was as dreary as the house. There were potholes on the one-lane road, half the street lights didn't work, and most of the buildings looked abandoned. Roving bands of teenagers passed by every now and then on their bicycles, their voices loud and their language coarse.

I thought at first that I was the only occupant of my building. But on the second day, the bell rang and I opened it to find an old woman on the doorstep. Age made her stoop and liver spots darkened the pale skin of her neck. She smiled with teeth that had to be dentures: white, pristine, and set in a neat row.

I live upstairs, she told me. Came by to welcome you to the neighbourhood and to give you this. I know that they don't let you keep a stove here. It's just ridiculous, if you ask me.

She handed me a casserole dish. It was heavy and I carried it over to the table, the old woman on my heels. I opened the lid and the aroma of some kind of cooked meat wafted out. I hope you like it, she said. I didn't eat meat but it was easier to lie and say that I would.

Don't hesitate to ask me any questions you might have about the neighbourhood, she continued. I'm always happy to help.

There was an expectant look on her face as she said this, as if she wanted me to ask her a question right away, and so I asked her where I could go to get some groceries.

The question delighted her. She proceeded to give me detailed instructions on how to get to the local supermarket and told me what to avoid in the produce aisle. The tomatoes, she said in a conspiratorial whisper, they are always old and rotten. Best stay away from them, okay?

I said okay, I would remember that, and she asked me then what my name was. She mangled up the pronunciation but told me that she would work on it. I didn't ask her for her name.

I saw the dog on the way to the supermarket, on a rubbish heap at the end of the street. A group of boys stood a little distance from her. They were taking turns to chuck small objects her way. Empty packets of cigarettes, twigs from a nearby hedge, mishappen pebbles. The dog ignored them and kept her head down, like this was a nuisance she couldn't be bothered to deal with.

When the boys spotted me, they fled, leaving behind a pile of the things they were going to throw next and the fading sound of their laughter. The dog remained in her crouched posture, seemingly unaware that her tormentors were no longer around.

She was still in the same position when I returned. I slowed down until I came to a halt not far from her spot. She was an unremarkable creature. Fawn coloured with splotches of black on the snout and the tail, one ear bent and the other straight, ribs that showed through the fur of her back. A thick cloud of flies floated above her head. The more enterprising of these insects landed on her from time to time, as if to check if she was still warm and alive or if she was ripe for the taking.

As I watched, the dog raised her head and her brown eyes met mine. She bared her teeth and a low growl thrummed in the rank air between us.

I took a step away but she remained where she was. I noticed then that there was something wrong with one of her front legs: the paw had turned inward at an odd angle. She looked as if she was sweeping the rubbish that she sat on towards herself – a dragon clutching its treasure horde close to its chest – and that I had disturbed her in the middle of this chore. She growled again, louder this time, and I walked away from there.

*

The man came by to tell me the date of the first interview, scheduled to take place later in the week. I no longer remembered his name, even though it had only been a couple of days since he had brought me to the house. All I remembered was that he had introduced himself as an agent. An agent of what? I wasn't sure.

He pointed at the sandwiches I had made and asked if he could help himself to one. I'm starving, he said as he picked up a triangle of bread, I've been running around since the morning. There are more of you every day.

Like on the previous occasion, he paused to see what I had to say to this. He wanted me to appear curious about these other people, perhaps ask him if any of them were staying nearby. I took a bite of my own sandwich and said nothing.

Now, he continued as if my silence didn't bother him, don't worry about the panel much, yeah? They look intimidating and all but they're people too. Remember that. And be sure to smile. A smile always helps. Why don't you go ahead and give me a smile now, the best one you've got?

I swallowed and parted my lips in the closest approximation of a smile that I could manage. He whistled and wiped his mouth. Those teeth, he said, you need to get them looked at. Here, let me give you the address of a dentist nearby.

He scribbled a name and address on a scrap of paper and put it on the table. These tomatoes, he pointed at his half-eaten sandwich, there's something wrong with them.

The dentist looked like me. I wanted to ask her how long she had been working there but it was difficult to speak with my mouth held open for her to examine my teeth. She tut-tutted after a few minutes. This is going to need a lot of work, she declared.

By the time our session ended, pain bloomed all along my jawline. I sat hunched on the chair and nursed my face in my hands like it was a delicate piece of pottery. The dentist peeled off her gloves and outlined the work that was still pending. Come after two weeks, she said in the end. Any questions?

The pain, I mumbled, will it go? Her brown eyes blinked and frown lines formed on her face, lines that disappeared behind the mask that she had not removed after the procedure.

I'll give you a prescription for painkillers, she said.

I sneaked out of the house in the middle of the night, my mouth still sore and with the casserole dish tucked under my arm. The dog was asleep but she gave a start when I approached her. She watched me with eyes wary under the moonlight as I removed the lid and upended the meat onto the ground, extending my arms to get the food as close to her as I could. I didn't wait to see if she would eat or if she would snarl at me again. I turned around and jogged back to the house.

There were three people on the panel, two men and a woman. They spent the interview talking to each other instead of asking me questions. I sat on a wooden chair and shivered in the cold draft that made its way into the room. The source of the wind puzzled me; there were no windows and the door through which I had entered remained shut.

It's a tricky case, you know, the woman said, and it took me a while to realize that she was talking to me at last. Our priority here is children and people with children.

The two men who sat on either side of her nodded. Families, she added, as if she wanted to clarify herself. You can see why we are reluctant to reach a decision right away. It would have been a no-brainer if you had a family.

If I had a family, I wouldn't be here. These words formed in my mouth and I deliberated on whether I should utter them out loud. The moment stretched on until the woman exhaled. Her breath came out as a puff of white mist which faded into the air before it could reach my chair.

We'll meet again, she said. In the meantime, do think about why you have a need for shelter and why we should consider your case.

Too late I remembered the agent's advice to smile more. I tried to do it then but my lips felt like strips of rubber, numb from the painkiller I had taken in the morning. It must have looked to the panelists as if I

*

I returned from the interview to find the old woman and the dog in a stand-off in the middle of the street. The woman held an unfurled umbrella before her like a sword. The dog stood by the door to the house, lop-sided as she leaned on her good foreleg.

Ah dear, my neighbour said when she spotted me. This creature here refuses to budge.

As if to demonstrate this, she waved her umbrella in a wide arc and said shoo. The dog remained calm but her eyes never left the old woman. I'll lead her away, I said.

I reached out a hand in the direction of the dog. Come here, I told her. She looked reluctant to tear her gaze away from the woman but she limped towards me anyway. When her nose was almost within touching distance of my hand, I turned around and walked away.

I didn't look back but I could hear her panting as she struggled to follow me. I kept walking until we reached the rubbish heap. Stay here, I told the dog. She sat on her haunches, a thread of drool stretching from her jowls to the ground. Stay, I said again and went back.

The old woman had opened the door to the house by then. Thank you, dear, she said. I can't abide these dogs. I really can't. They carry fleas on them.

I nodded and looked down the road, half-expecting the limping form of the dog to reappear. You had a way with that thing, the woman added before trudging up the stairs to her flat, it seemed to understand you.

*

The agent told me that he had seen the transcript of my interview and that it didn't look promising. You didn't speak at all, he said, you sat there and didn't say a word. I bet you didn't smile either.

I shrugged away his admonishment. He frowned at me and then looked at the empty casserole dish on the table. You seem to be making friends at least, he said. In the next interview, you should talk about that, about how you're becoming a part of the neighbourhood. That'll make a good impression.

He took a half-step towards the door before turning to me again. You should also think of an alternative name, he said, something you like the sound of. Never hurts to show that you're eager to be here.

*

The dog was back on her spot atop the rubbish heap. Her ear, the straight one, had blood all over it. A dented tin of condensed milk – the missile that struck her – lay by her paws. She licked at the dregs that seeped out of it and pretended to ignore me as I went past her.

I tried to talk to the dentist about this but she was not interested. Keep your mouth open please, she told me, we'll be here all day otherwise.

*

I lead the dog back to the house under the cover of the night's darkness. It was easier than I had anticipated; she seemed to bear no grudge against me for tricking her earlier. She followed with her slow, painful steps and we took several breaks on the short walk over to let her rest.

I spread a bedsheet in a corner of the bedroom – the one with the least amount of mould clinging to its surface – and told the dog to lie down on it. She obeyed me and then proceeded to lick her belly with long, patient strokes of her tongue. Mud covered her underside, from the nook between her forelegs to her distended teats.

Where are your pups? I asked her.

She stopped licking and fixed me with a steady but impenetrable gaze. Her whole body was still except for the damaged paw, which trembled a little as if caught in a stiff breeze.

I moved my hand closer to her paw and she sneezed, a loud and very human sneeze that made her entire body shudder violently. I waited for her to become still again before touching her paw with an index finger. She whined and jerked her leg away.

That must be painful, I told her. And that.

I pointed at her ear, where the blood had now dried. She followed my finger with her eyes and didn't make any other sound.

I crushed my nightly dose of the painkiller and fed it to the dog along with a slice of bread. Then I dragged my mattress to the other end of the room and settled down to sleep.

The dog keened once in the middle of the night. I woke up and shivered under my blanket as the sound of her crying slipped into my bones. I considered tiptoeing across the room to comfort her but in the end, I didn't.

I opened the door only a crack when my neighbour rang the bell the next day. I wanted to get you more food, she said, but you still have my casserole dish. If you give it to me, I'll bring you something hot to eat for lunch.

Wait here, I said. I closed the door and went to the table to retrieve her utensil. Here, I slipped it through the door, and you don't need to get me anything more. I'm good, thanks.

Her smile dimmed a little and the effect this had on her face was startling. She looked older than she ever had before, her face sunken and shapeless like a melted candle. It's no bother to me, she said, bringing you more food, that is. I like to do it.

Please, I told her, no. I don't want any more food.

She hugged the empty casserole dish to her chest and looked at her tattered slippers. Say, she asked, did you hear any strange noises last night? I thought I heard crying.

No, I told her, I didn't hear anything.

*

The next knock on the door came from the agent. He looked agitated when I opened the door. You missed the interview, he said. How could you do that?

He gritted his teeth and stomped his foot. His teeth, I noticed, were in bad shape. There were tobacco stains on them and at least two of his canines were chipped. Well? He asked. Are you not going to let me in or what?

I looked over my shoulder and saw that the dog had emerged from the bedroom to investigate the source of the noise. It's not a good time, I said.

The man's eyes bulged. Not a good time? Not a fucking good time? What are you, the fucking Queen?

I shrugged. He took a few deep breaths to calm himself down. Listen man, he said, you need to let me in. Your neighbour? That kind old lady upstairs? She called me this morning, said she heard strange noises from your flat. I wanted to come talk to you after the interview but then I found out that you skipped the bloody thing.

We stared at each other for a while before I relented and opened the door wider. He took a step inside and the first thing he saw was the dog.

Fuck, he murmured. It's a dog.

I went and sat on the chair. As if taking her cue from me, the dog also sat down and gathered her head into the fold of her bent paw, licking the fur over her leg.

This isn't allowed, the man told me. You know this, right? It's against the rules.

I know, I said.

He looked like he had more things to say but some part of him must have recognized the futility of it for he sighed and leaned back against the front door.

I'm sorry, he said, for swearing at you earlier.

That's okay.

He waved a hand in the direction of the dog. Does it have a name?

I looked at the dog and she stopped licking her paw to meet my eyes. No, I said, she doesn't.

Annie Q. Syed

Annie Q. Syed is a reader and writer who teaches full time. Her novel was a runner-up for the Irish Writers Centre's Novel Fair 2021 and the Blue Pencil Agency's 2020 Pitch Prize. Her essays and fiction have appeared in *The Common Breath, Zeno Press, The Fiddlehead, The Honest Ulsterman, Tahoma Literary Review, Afreada*, and in *Bath Flash Fiction* and *Reflex Fiction* anthologies. Sometimes she blogs and shares photos at www. anniesyed.com.

This is How You Lie

he first lie always happens at 8:30am because I can't make it to Language Arts class on time. I hate that minute when I give Ms. Nora my late pass which says "Unexcused Tardy" and she glances away, as if looking at me too long will reveal all my lies to myself and I would feel ashamed. She's nice like that; doesn't like to shame anyone. Or maybe that's a lie I like to believe about her, maybe she is like all the other adults, only thinking about themselves.

There are supposed to be people in school who check why you haven't been there. That's something that only happens in the movies. In those shows if your parents have money they can get a doctor's note; some heroes write their own fake notes. But in real life, if your handwriting looks like you're still in grade school (because you are), you better get good at lying. Sometimes I don't know if I lie for my father or for myself.

It's hard to lie in a small town where everyone knows everyone's business. It's the kind of town where truth tastes like dry heat, even a breezy day feels like asphalt and truck mufflers blowing on your skin. Truth is heavy to swallow here. Lies, on the other hand, happen like breathing. It doesn't matter who the lying is for, but here is the recipe to not get caught.

You can't think twice before lying. No extra blinks, lip licks, inhales-exhales. Let the words slip from your tongue. *I went away with my father on a business trip.* This is a good one because it can be to faraway places. And because everyone knows you don't have a mother, they understand why your father can't leave you at home. Or at least they know why he shouldn't.

Don't make the lie so big that it creates a splash. The plop from your lie should be directly proportional to the truth. Don't go naming LA or NYC as your destination; everyone knows they are far away and for the rich. When the farthest your teacher has travelled is the Uptown Mall, come up with real places within driving distance but ones she has never heard of. Crownpoint. Blackrock. Crocker. Grady. You get the idea.

Best to stick within the range of previous lies. If you start lying big, then you may start believing your own lies, and that can make you resent yourself. I know what resent means; it's the way a person turns on themselves for believing something that's never going to happen. You are never going camping, fishing, or visiting Grandpa. Don't believe your lies so much that you become your father. He is not like Jay's dad who drinks too much. He is not like the character from a book you are reading in class, where the father beats his son. But he does believe his own lies, especially the one about "becoming so rich that we wouldn't know whattado with all the money." He gets sad on those days he realizes it hasn't happened and may never happen. He never gets angry at me even when he is disappointed. Only in himself; then he doesn't speak for a long time.

Good to have someone like Ms. Nora on your side. A teacher like her is exactly the kind of grown up who will never question your lies, someone who knows you are lying but feels bad about calling you out on it. "Out of town for work, again?" Slow nod twice and smile. She is the type of adult who genuinely cares; spruce up your lie by connecting it with the learning in class to make her feel appreciated for caring. "They had trees there, those big weepy willow kind, just like in that poem we read."

Once you start, you can't stop, my father says, but he doesn't mean lying when he says that. "I'm not ashamed; besides, you think I care what anyone in this town thinks of me? People who care what others think are never going to have good luck."

I know that's not wisdom, but I believe him anyway.

He says things that make sense – if you don't think about them. Lies make sense too if you don't think about them.

"There isn't really a way out of this town without money. And it's not like I don't work hard. And it's a hard day's work every day." He ruffles the hair on top of my head before he drops me at school. He usually does that when he hasn't said much to me in a few days because he is doubting himself.

I know he is telling the truth; it isn't safe to leave me alone at night when he goes to his second job. That's what he calls it. Although sometimes he loses money instead of making it.

For a long time my formula worked like a charm.

Then one day, out of nowhere, my presentation must have got too elaborate for Ms. Nora to believe.

"No, we weren't out of town for my dad's work," I had said. I changed it up a bit. I think it was because I hadn't slept enough and didn't think about what I was saying.

This time she didn't look away. "Are you okay?"

"Yeah. Just tired."

When she continued to ignore students' chatter instead of telling them to be quiet or open the novel or even give them a look, I knew I had slipped and forgotten the formula.

"We were at the drive-in movies." I didn't even know how those worked but that's what I had said. "They were over late. And then we had a drive."

"Where is this drive-in?" She kept looking at me.

I did the worst thing you can do when lying: I shrugged. It was over then.

She told the principal who did nothing; she told his secretary who did nothing. She found me at lunch and she told me she even called the district; apparently, all schools have to answer to this place called district. She told me all this to show me that what she was about to do next – call my father – was because she was concerned about me.

My father missed her calls over the next few days and I continued being late so she actually showed up at our house. I couldn't decide if I was having bad luck or good luck. My father had just left for work at the autobody repair shop – for a small town we have a lot of accidents – much later than usual because at night we were out till 5am Someone owed him money, that's why it took longer, he'd said. Forget late; I never went to school.

Ms. Nora was at the door. I couldn't say her name out loud. People don't look the same everywhere. Standing there, she looked like a woman, a mom even.

"Hi." She peeked over and around me to see if anyone else was home. "The principal knows I am here. You didn't come to school today and I have been worried about you given how you are chronically late."

"Nothin's wrong." I sounded confident so she didn't worry, but lying at school is different than lying at home. I should have spoken louder and clearer and not been looking at her shoes.

"Where is your father?"

"At work." It was the truth.

"So you are by yourself?"

"I didn't feel good today." Her shoes were black and looked worn like our couch.

"Listen – today it's me, but someone from the district is going to eventually do a welfare check, okay? This..." She eyed around behind me again. Our house was always clean, dad made sure of that. I wondered what she thought of that. "This is not okay. You need to be in school."

"Why?" I hadn't meant to sound angry; I liked her.

"It's the law."

Lots of things were the law and it didn't make a difference. I wondered if her explanation sounded like a lie to her.

I decided to come clean with her. It's hard to lie to someone who cares. It was the first time I felt there was a difference between not lying and telling the truth. But I cared about my father more.

New recipe:

Make sure the first 1/3 of your lie is truthful. *I was with my dad.*

The next 1/3 is the lie. *He runs his own business.*

The final 1/3 must be based on a past no one remembers and a future no one you know will be part of. No one will ever meet your father. They won't ask why your mother left him because then they have to ask themselves what kind of mother leaves her own kid. No one is brave enough to admit the truth: your dad is just not the responsible grown-up type. This final 1/3 is where you can say almost anything because no one is really listening that far into the lie because they are thinking of their own reasons to not bring up the truth. They are comfortable saying Jay's dad is a drunk and Ms. Nora will help you analyze the abusive father in the story you all are reading in class, but no one is going to question someone like your father. Because he isn't really doing anything wrong. During the final 1/3 you can say, *He takes me to places with big flashing lights on the outside, like a theme park that's only open at night.* You know that sorta thing. Make it wild. No one is listening to the final bit.

Only you will know it's the kind of place where kids are not allowed. They have dice and cards and noisy slot machines inside. Everything in there has to do with luck and a lot can go wrong when it comes to luck. It's the kind of place where outside in the parking lot there's only you, your book, your flashlight and extra batteries.

Walking from the receptionist's desk at the entrance of the school building through the long corridors to Ms. Nora's classroom always reminds me of the rides home with my father. It's dark on the highways then and there are no cars and you can't wait to get home even if there is no difference between sleeping in the car or at home. But sleeping inside a car is like sleeping in a box; you know it's not the place for resting.

Yes, Ms. Nora, you say, *I did my homework.* That's the truth.

Danielle Vrublevskis

Danielle Vrublevskis was born in Germany, grew up in Bristol and now lives in London. She's worked as a researcher, bookseller, and translator, both in the UK and in Beijing and Hong Kong. When she's not writing, she can be found trying to coax her balcony tomato plants back to life.

The Carnivore Club

Any other gals struggle with the blood? Loving all-meat journey so far, tho.

Stupid first post. Needy, weak, full of complaint. I clicked my question onto the group and then put my phone away for half an hour before returning to the responses:

I did at first x.

Try eating it medium rare. Don't go from 0-60. Ramp up, hun.

I didn't need their well wishes – lovely messages for condolence cards, valentine cards, birthday cards – I didn't need anything that might fit on a card.

You a vegan or something?

No. Just new to the diet.

Try harder.

I clicked onto the profile of the woman who had posted this. Rebekah. Steaks, seared only on the outside, ruddy with flavour. Burgers, flushed and beckoning. Jumbled anatomy spread out on a platter for a barbeque held on a sunny day in Luton, only two hours' travel away from me.

She was an estate agent. Pallid husband, and a little boy glimpsed in the background of photos. I clicked through every image to see the transformation in her:

Before: flabby, dry hair, slow eyes, worried (probably about climate change or infidelity).

After: muscled, clear skin, gaze direct at the camera and legs astride like she owned every pixel on my screen, like she'd burst right on through the fuzziness of 1,080p to 2,160p maybe all the way to 4,320p. So confident with the After that screen resolutions couldn't contain her.

I resolved to become After.

I saw Rebekah next at a meetup. Just us gals, it was, twenty or so women in the top room of a pub, sipping vodka and gin, ordering burgers and steaks. The searing was alright on my burger, but the ground beef was cheap, reminded me of the stuff I bought by the kilo for meals: meatballs, nuggets, pancakes. We all left our salads and microwaved carrots aside like last year's bikinis.

When we arrived, there'd been enough of the male gaze on us to fill an art museum, but now we were left alone. There was a presentation on aged meats: one woman had travelled to Texas for a 459-day aged steak. She said it smelled a bit like blue cheese, that the skin tasted like rocks.

I need another shit, I say halfway through. They all nod in sympathy. It isn't a new phrase, it's a joke for the whole group. You can even buy it on a T-shirt.

I'd read the warnings about the diarrhoea ahead of time. Thought I knew what to expect, thought I could control it all, but now have incontinence pads in my regular shop and my algorithm can't decide if I'm a meat-loving alpha-male or a frail old woman with bowel issues. I've ordered up some beef liver crisps, to make up for the malnutrition and hopefully solve the problem. You can get all your vitamins from meat, you just need to be disciplined.

When I came out of the toilet stall, that's when I saw Rebekah again: woman/After. I took a while washing my hands so that she had to use the sink next to me.

It's only my second time, I said.

Keep at it sport, she said. She had hair large and lustrous enough for a 70s film. She was the kind of woman that bankers offered coke to.

Well, that's the thing, I said. I need some help.

Ignore the GP advice, get to know your local butcher. It's really not that difficult, she said. Her voice was full of butter.

She was leaving the bathroom now, heading out. I'd switched her mode from sorta-interested to sorta-not. Another woman stood queuing in the doorway, bowing her head to her phone, drunk, not paying attention. Rebekah tried to get past her, but the woman didn't notice in time, and they bumped shoulders. It wasn't much, but the woman looked up from her phone and said, watch it cow, and Rebekah turned and oh yes, here she'd go into the big knockout, but she only rolled her eyes and moved on.

I followed her out, and the door-woman didn't move for me either. People generally don't – I have hotel art aura. My father (1960-2021) said I could be an international assassin because nobody would ever remember me, then laughed like it was a new joke.

So I walked past door-woman then, oh no, I knocked the phone out of her hand and said, ooops, just like they do in movies, all exaggerated and the loudest I've ever heard my voice. Heard Rebekah giggle.

You don't really think about ever getting punched. It's not in the list of options available, not in the outcomes of a day. So it was a big surprise when it happened.

You know what you need? asked Rebekah.

Don't say a frozen steak. Everywhere is shut, I said. Rebekah's car smelled of mint.

Fine, she said. Frozen peas.

Very funny, I said. Not letting that shit anywhere near my face, thanks very much, kindly. I pulled the tissue away from my eye.

How am I looking?

Pulverised.

In a good way? I asked and she laughed. The bleeding near my eyebrow had stopped. I'd have a black eye.

Work going to be an issue? Asked Rebekah. She shuffled closer to examine the damage. Will they ask you what you've been up to at your weekends?

Not a problem.

So they won't ask you anything about this? Her breath was sour. The kiss made my cheek hurt and I said, wait, but I don't think she heard and so I just let it go on until she got tired and said, you know, it's late, and there are husbands and children to think about, you probably have them too let's not bring them up, eh? Other people and so on.

This place is the tits, she said. Sometimes, when she spoke, she took on an American accent. Maybe she'd learned it from the television (the shows she liked: sitcoms with lessons at the end, cooking shows where they all hated each other), or maybe she had come over as a child and never assimilated. We'd been seeing each other for a few months now, and I hadn't figured it out.

It's the tits, she said. The best you've ever had, think of that, then multiply it by ten. Then by another ten.

Sounds pretty good, I said. The best I'd ever eaten had been a fast food burger, ordered after my father's funeral, me still in my all black but nobody giving a shit. Nobody to tell me off for leaving the gherkins uneaten. So it would maybe be a hundred times better than that burger.

It's paradise, darling, she said. Disneyland, but not neutered. The pigs, they can't wait to be slaughtered.

There was a list that she'd got us both on. The restaurant was small, just enough room for a dozen or so. All black on the outside, and full of metal on the inside and there weren't any windows, even though it was on the ground floor. Glass screen between us and the chefs, so we could see them dismantle the carcasses, archaeologists unpicking the meat, scholars of flavour.

Lots of flooding here, said Rebekah, so they probably don't want to put in a basement, as great as that would be.

She liked to show off when she knew stuff. Mainly about buildings, and how much they were worth.

A descent would have been nice, instead of just a step over a threshold but either way we went down and were soon three beers deep, sharing a platter of meats (assorted, serves 4 but we were only 2). Our laughter was high and piercing over the bassy music they played on a loop, getting us looks from the other patrons (bearded, bearded, tattoo + bearded, no beard but big glasses – a big bunch of Befores if I ever saw one).

When we finished, they asked us if we wanted desserts and Rebekah shook her head, we don't eat that shit.

Fair enough, said too-skinny waiter. It seems to be working. This said to her, not me.

When he went and got the bill, she leaned in and said like it was a secret, can you believe the cheek?

I said that I couldn't, though of course I could, had seen it happen every time we went out together, she knew that too, of course she did.

The cheek of him, the cheek, I said. The jowl and tongue and beard of him.

I tried talking to Rebekah about a recipe I'd found for carnivore cake: just eggs, butter and a bit of vanilla. Maybe we could try it? But she was distracted, watching the waiter.

When he came back, he was so tense his shoulders were halfway up to his ears. He leaned to speak to Rebekah and I heard declined, alternative card, cash, heavy words that he tried to lighten.

What do you mean it's declined? she said. Loud, embarrassing. Check again. Try this one instead. You have anything on you?

I shook my head. Not enough to cover this meal, and I couldn't afford to go into my overdraft again.

She began to cry. Fuck, she said. That fucking asshole. Stifled a sob, wiped her tears quickly, like she was embarrassed. It's my husband, she said. He's done this before, tried to control me. Can I give you anything? An email address, a phone number? I have the money, I promise, I just need to unblock the account.

Too-thin waiter hesitated.

I've got this, I said. Took out a tenner from my purse, laid it on the table. Just to start with?

He shrugged, then let Rebekah give him her details. I didn't look, knew she wouldn't like it (privacy is the most valuable asset, you think billionaires go around handing their details to everybody who wants it?).

Then, when we were out of the restaurant and back in her car, I said, Is everything okay? At home?

For a second she paused. Eyes brown, still swimming like somebody had thrown chilli in them and rubbed, marinated until they got the tears. Then she laughed. Of course, she said. He doesn't even know about this card. Sweet man, but dumb as they come. She looked fondly at me, then reached over and pinched my arm where it was most fleshy.

That's for giving in, she said. You didn't need to hand over that tenner.

She pinched again, pinking my skin. And that's for the onions. I saw you looking at them, like you wanted to eat them.

Sorry, I said, and she kissed me and said, of course you are, but be better next time my darling, my love and I took that word love into the hotel room, into the next month. Every time she texted I made sure I answered.

Meet me at the usual place, she messaged me. Hurry.

I booked the room under my name, like I always did. A city across from where she lived. Much further for me, but I didn't mind that so much. High enough turnover that the bar staff at the hotel didn't recognise us or maybe they had never cared in the first place, no need to think everyone is watching, that everybody cares, insignificant blip on a pale blue dot etc.

But it was still nice to be treated as a stranger. I dressed up, black business skirt and white shirt like I was a professional during the day. Rebekah always came in something bright and patterned, and I liked to complement her, my binaries against her multitudes.

I almost didn't recognise her when she turned up in grey (Grey? Brown? Navy? A colour so worn down it lost its identity and made you search around for new ones).

Oh, you're here, she said. 50% sad, 50% relieved, was how I judged it.

Why wouldn't I be?

Just one of those days, she said. You know. Whisky, one for us both.

Double, yeah. Do you really need to ID me? I'm thirty-seven, well yes, yes it's a compliment, here's my license.

I caught her picture, briefly shown, and her address. Familiar to me.

We talked about our progress, the weight I'd lost and put on in the right places, how clean and fresh we both were, how totally pinnacle the diet had made us – not gatherers but hunters only. We saw with hunter eyes, caught glimpses of prey in shop windows, dreamt of chasing down deer.

Then, halfway through the drink, she said, it's my kid. My boy. He's being bullied and I keep telling him to stand up, to be a man, but he just won't.

What?

And I've told the husband and he said let the teachers handle it, but I'm not going to have some child of mine being a loser. And if he's like this now, what about in a few years' time?

Her voice lost any richness, became thin and miserly, like she was counting out every word and logging them later in a spreadsheet. I don't know what to do, she said.

Let's eat first, I said. A proper meal will help. Then we can go to the room, relax.

I don't want to go to the room. Weren't you listening, I've got a life to sort out? My kid –

Okay, I said. Just a meal, first.

It wasn't much, to tell the truth. We asked for the steaks rare and they came out medium rare and when we sent them back there was a right scene and by the time they'd made us a new one my stomach ached and Rebekah had needed the toilet three times. But cavemen didn't complain did they when they were hungry for all that mammoth meat and so I, feeling pretty strong, said,

Listen, about Jack. Get him into a boxing class or something. Toughen your son up. Otherwise, these bullies will never learn.

Yeah, she said. Yeah, I keep telling him to go but he won't.

She hooked a sprig of rosemary on her fork and removed it from the top of the steak, precise and clinical (MeatEater MD – her a jaded surgeon, me a bright-eyed young intern).

I asked for no greens, she said. I thought she would make another complaint but she didn't, just left it there on the side of her plate.

When we went up to the room I'd booked (always the fourth floor, high enough to be away from any eyes but low enough that I could get out quickly), she produced a bottle of whisky from her bag. She gave a flourish, Houdini in her eyes, selling the magic to you even as she told you it wasn't real. Only difference is, I reckoned she would survive that punch to the stomach. All those sit ups she did, she had abs that defied sudden, tragic death, abs that I saw shifting underneath her skin as she unhooked her bra.

She got drunker that night than I had ever seen her before.

We can wait, I said. Till tomorrow.

No, she said. Now, it has to be right now.

I hesitated.

Come on, she said. Pinched my arm, my thigh. Laughed at the goosebumps all over my body, how plucked I looked.

I kissed up her legs, tasted salt from the heat of the day. Nipped that immortal stomach and felt her tense and heard her moan, as she always did. Did it again, harder, and this time she flinched.

Ow, she said. Stop. Stop.

She shuffled back, frowning at me.

Think I did have too much, she said. She picked up her underwear and shuffled it on. Let's just go to sleep.

Sure, I said. Sure, okay, fine.

The sound of next door's TV came through the walls. Somebody beeped their horn outside, and a strip club played discrete R&B. There was lemon and lime on my tongue, god knows from where. The cleaning products, maybe.

Then I said, guess weakness runs in the family.

She did hurt so well, lips pouting, arms crossed over her chest. It was all a bit much. You need practice to be good at performing wounded and she didn't have it. Though she was, I have to admit, a rising star in the genre. Then all this pain, it turned.

Earlier on, she said, looking at me like I was behind glass. You said Jack, about my son. How did you know? I don't tell women his name.

You told me.

No, she said. I never do.

Never?

She didn't say much after that, turning the light on while I was still checking my socials and letting me get all that nasty blue light in my brain. I had trouble sleeping and when I woke up she'd already left the room, along with all her luggage.

I left the next morning after a quick trip to the breakfast buffet, filling my pockets with napkin-wrapped sausages and bacon strips.

She was outside the reception, next to the now-shuttered strip bar. She had a cigarette in her hand (the smell didn't hang about her, so it must have been a lapse into an old habit, a habit that predated any of her social media), and she was talking on the phone, to a driver who had no idea where she was, but she'd put in the postcode right, no it wasn't a house it was a hotel, don't you even know where the hotels are?

Then, she stubbed out her cigarette, and, brazenly, hussily, unscrewed a bottle of orange juice. I watched her drink it in less than a minute. Poor dear, like she was a traveller coming across an oasis.

Right, I said. Right, I see.

She turned around, hung up her phone.

Oh, she said. It's you.

That's full of junk, I said. Sugar, empty calories.

She looked down at the juice.

Oh, she said. Yeah, I was thirsty.

No, I said. You're doing it wrong. There's meats that will give you the vitamins: liver, offal. No, no, I know what's making you do this. Bile acid malabsorption.

What?

Didn't you read that article I posted on the group? 10 ways to solve carnivore diet gut?

No. She tipped the drink up again, getting those last drops, then said, it's not a big deal.

It is, I said.

Grow up, said Rebekah. I'm not perfect, nobody is. That's why we come together in the Carnivore Club, not to pick each other apart, but to build each other up.

She turned it on so quickly, even though there was no audience. Even though it was just us two. Eyes fierce, hair shimmering behind her as if she'd arranged for a wind machine, all music-video power stances and just that bit of vulnerability. I almost bought it, and she saw my hesitation, knew it for what it was.

Women supporting women, she said. Not tearing them down.

A car pulled up, tentatively. Her ride to the station, and she'd be away in a few minutes.

Well, I said, that shit doesn't seem to be helping your son, does it? I see what they post about him on socials.

Don't you –

He's a beta, your Jack. A victim, if I ever saw one.

She looked, for a moment, scared.

You don't come anywhere near me, alright? Never again.

Rebekah got into the taxi as quick as I'd ever seen her move, throwing her bag in. I messaged her, but the number pinged back immediately. A quick block, like she'd done it before.

On the coach home, I pulled out the bacon from my pocket and chewed my way through it. The girl next to me crinkled up her face and made all these gestures but never touched me, didn't say anything, and I knew she would never. She knew she would lose if it came to a fight, that girl (a Before), and that I would win (an After).

I clicked onto a page, switched my profile picture. Someone gentler, a bit posher. She wore glasses.

I'm still trying this diet, I said. Struggling with the social judgement and staying strong when there's vegetables all around. You can't move for vegan restaurants!

Keep at it! There's plenty of us rooting for you.

Anna Whyatt

Anna Whyatt is a writer, sculptor, and dramaturg. She has worked for many years in creative/cultural fields nationally and in Europe, including work with Tate Modern, the UK Film Council, an award-winning production at Chelsea Flower Show and advising at UK Ministerial and Shadow Cabinet level. She has been shortlisted and longlisted for several national and international literary competitions. Her sculpture has been shown in the UK, America and Poland, including a group exhibition sponsored by the V&A. Her published non-fiction covers articles, two books and ten years as a columnist for a national magazine.

On Drowning

Even my name was not actually mine. Plucked, my mother swore in a more rational moment from her died-in-infancy sister. Believe that if you like. But once told, I never felt I owned myself. Just a shadow replacement for someone else.

Afterwards I saw that was no great surprise. Everything we owned scrounged or thrown out by other people. The tin bath (borrowed from one of the other cowmen) like a shiny salamander hanging on the scullery nail and fetched down for bath night each week beside the faded rag rug (thrown out by the big house up the lane) the kitchen table, the tins for tea and sugar (cast-offs from the village shop) then painted blue with paint from the barn. Our hats and coats, the creaking bicycle our father wheeled out every morning to collect the milk (his mate's brother's). Our parents accepted anything thrown at them. A collar for the cat, a moth-eaten jersey, its wool unravelled to re-knit into scarves, chipped blue and white cups, the odd picture of Swiss mountains lacking its glass hung on the upstairs walls.

We'd been playing with the family two fields away from us. I was at that stage with my family that I knew as long as I kept moving, everything could be made to be fine.

Besides, the Mulveys were Irish. Even lower down the pecking order than we were. Safety in numbers. Their four girls were older. Bossy. With queer kind of dominance over my brother and me. Petting and fussing over us. Dressing us in shawls and odd bits of fur to become servants bearing trays. Extras watching their plays on words. Pouting at themselves in the mirror, as they tried on lipstick borrowed from their mam's bag when she was out.

We'd played all morning and were late starting back for dinner. By then the Mulvey girls had also got into the business of donating. Lugging down the thing we'd always envied – the doll's house they'd grown out of in the back bedroom. The doll's house wasn't large, just wooden, and heavy. The youngest Mulvey daughter and I had stopped to rest, my brother trailing behind. A shadow fell over us. Our father come to find out where we were. He seized the doll's house with unusual exasperation, 'This – is going right back.'

Then he asked me who I thought we were. I didn't answer. I knew even then it was a figure of speech question. I'd thought we were people who'd be grateful for anything. On this occasion, as it now turned out, I was wrong.

After that, no more visits to the Mulveys. Resentfully obedient, I couldn't understand why. One of those adult mysteries. But even then, I had a suspicion it had something to do with status. Accepting cast offs from those wealthier uplifted you somehow, made you more worthy. Donations from lower orders meant being brought down to their level. A first lesson in degrees of social standing. Later, when things got more shameful, I thought perhaps if I'd refused the doll's house, we might have got off more lightly. At least we'd have started off a little higher on the shelf of social standing before we finally tipped right over.

We open our eyes. There's no indication before this day will be different from any other. But the next minute, it's obvious. For one thing it's our father, normally out working by the time we wake, who rouses us, not our mother. Hurrying us into our clothes, cack-handed buttoning up of sweaters normally kept for Sundays, jamming on socks and knickers under skirts and trousers too thin for this time of year. Secondly instead of sitting us down to breakfast, taking down cups, pouring out milk, we're hurried out the door and up the long lane. It's only just light. But you can make out the vetches and wildflowers already lining the hedgerows, the flat lemon faces of primroses lingering in their shadow. The dried mud from last week's rain ridged and sharp under our Wellington boots.

The final nail in the coffin of the ordinary comes when we're taken into the gardens of the big house where our father sometimes works. Past the box hedges, the neat squares of rose beds where we normally wait to the back door and into the kitchen. I pull my hair over the bruise on my forehead. And it must be because my head's already down, dying of embarrassment, that the first thing I notice is the floor. Not like anything I've seen before: sparkling black and white tiles, clean enough to eat off. The high table and chairs shiny from polish. The glorious yellow yolk of the boiled eggs put in front of us. Toast without crusts, cut into pieces like fingers. '*Soldiers*' the girl in the white apron who makes the breakfast calls them. We don't know what she's talking about.

But we don't care. We're in Paradise. We eat slowly, savouring the yellow yolk, the perfectly cooked white. We know they're eggs just fetched from the hen house because round the edge of mine, exactly moulded to the shape of the egg, there's a small feather, brown fading through beige to white. I peel it away from the shell and put it into my skirt pocket. I'm scared of losing it, it's so light. Even a cough would blow it away. I look up. The sheepdog drowsing in a basket by the long black stove watches me, his eyes sharply interested. For an instant, I feel like a thief. But it's only a feather. Surely in all that crowd of belongings, they won't miss it. Later, while we wait for our father's return, we're allowed to pet the sheepdog, stroke the soft top of his head.

Our father comes back. We leave Paradise and walk back down the lane. Our father looks the same but somehow different. He holds my hand and carries my brother just like every day. But he doesn't joke or point out the pheasant in the grass beyond the pond or the white rose blooming by the kitchen door. In fact, he doesn't speak at all. We walk back into normal life. Back to our house, the only one for miles at the end of the lane. Looking out over the fields and the brown river, with only the barn and the oast house for company. We walk through the gate, the overgrown garden, past the swing our father made for us, (wood gleaned from last year's privy demolition) past the two rose trees, one white and one red, the rows of marigolds just emerging (last year's seeds from the woman who drives the butcher's van). It must still be early. I look up at the hornet moon showing through the grey blue patches of cloud.

At the top of the path, men in caps stand outside our back door, smoking and talking. Some of them known to us, others strangers. They wear rubber boots. And the trousers of two of them are sopping wet, as if they've been out in a storm. That's when I notice that our father's trousers are also soaked up to the waist. I get a queer feeling in my stomach that reaches up into my head as if I've swallowed the day whole. The men don't look at us. One of them stubs out his cigarette, 'We put the kettle on,' he says. In times like these, always the best thing.

We're lifted onto the bed to embrace our mother, her hair tied back with a fuchsia bow. The only colour I see in all that darkness. We know, looking at our father's face, that we're supposed to feel sorry. But what I feel most is relief at no more raging and beating for a bit. And anger. That we've been torn away from our glimpse of Paradise. That she came back.

Downstairs the men are leaving. Our father's mate drains his mug of the last of the tea and sets it on the table, 'Lucky we found her when we did, Jack. Before she got out any further. Ten minutes more, current would have done for her. Damn fast that river this time of year. What possessed her, walking in like that. In nightclothes. Why would she do that?'

We keep our heads down. You can think all kinds of things.

Maybe we could tell him.

But we won't.

David Winstone

David Winstone is a Writer/Director from the UK whose short film, For Elsie won the 2012 Student Academy Award. This led to a David Lean scholarship to study at the National Film & Television School, where he made more award-winning short films. He has also written several short stories including *When the Bird Sings*, which has been selected for The Blackwater Press Short Story Collection 2021. Recently he has been working in television on shows such as Hard Sun, River City, and Gangs of London.

The Parasol

My wife asked me to put the parasol away in the mini shed before tea time. She actually called it a 'garden umbrella' but I stopped correcting her a long time ago. Not only is she technically incorrect, as any umbrella can be used in the garden, she's also being inefficient, wasting words, but then she would almost certainly retort that I'm wasting even more words by correcting her and making a big deal out of it. I know this because it's happened before on several occasions. Anyway, the point is I forgot to put away the parasol and now I'm bleeding to death.

We woke up very early the next morning to a knock at the door. Vanessa and I argued for some time over whether to ignore it, but the knocking continued. The subject of the argument naturally progressed to who should answer it. I won't bore you with the details but I lost. I checked through the spy hole and saw a tall man with sad, tired eyes. He looked as though he might have been crying. He was holding a bright yellow parasol with white polka dots that looked exactly like ours. I hesitated at opening the door at first because dealing with emotional strangers is not what I like to do first thing on a Sunday morning but if it was somehow our parasol, I wanted it back.

"Is this yours?" he said instantly, in a quiet, worn out voice with a foreign accent I couldn't place. He read my confusion. "It landed in my garden late last night, I've been asking all around the neighbourhood for hours now..." It was then I remembered that it was actually quite stormy last night. That was part of the reason Vanessa wanted me to put the parasol away, the wind picked up and the clouds were grey, plus the app on her phone told her that a storm was coming and she didn't want another 'garden umbrella' ruined. "It's yours, isn't it?" He said gravely. I explained that it could well be but we would need to investigate the garden to find out for certain.

Even though it takes slightly longer we went around the side of the house rather than through it. I told him it was so we didn't wake up my wife but really I was just delaying the news to her that yes, I hadn't put the parasol away and yes, it did end up in another person's garden over a mile away and yes, I had fucked up yet again. We finally got to the garden and walked over to the well and truly parasol-less table. I apologised and explained that I must have forgotten to put it away last night and that now my wife was going to kill me, honest mistake, sorry about that, I said whilst half-chuckling in that definitely English 'existence is embarrassing, isn't it?' Way. That's when I noticed his hands were covered in blood. He stabbed the parasol down through the hole in the table, then steadied himself on the back of a chair, barely able to stand. Emotion started to pour out of him in what became like a scene from one of those Spanish films I don't like but The Guardian kept making me watch.

"My wife was out in the garden last night doing the ironing. She does the ironing in the garden you see, even when the weather is as bad as it was last night, we do this to keep my son safe. No matter how wet, how strong the wind, we do this. You see my son has... Problems. Big problems. He's not right. So anything he can use to hurt himself or others must be kept away. That is absolutely essential. We played rock paper scissors to decide who would do the ironing and who would put my son, Titus, to bed. I lost. I was padlocking Titus's door when I started to smell something burning. Do you know what burnt hair smells like? I do. I ran downstairs to the garden… And found this!"

He stabbed the parasol dramatically through the hole in the table again and again in anger. He was now choking on his tears.

"This fucking… Garden Umbrella. Was through my wife's neck. It must have been carried up by the storm and fallen from the sky like a lightning bolt from Zeus! She was lying there on the floor… And she must have knocked over the Ironing board on her way down… And… And the iron landed flat on her beautiful face! Now it's… Melted. I can only hope that the garden umbrella gave her a swift death before the iron fell!"

I decided not to correct him even though he kept calling it a garden umbrella.

"The thing is, the reason I'm here, is that well… I don't have the courage to tell my boy… I don't suspect Titus is capable of love, but if he is, if there is one thing he… It was her… And since this is your garden umbrella…"

"It's the least you could do Pete. I did tell him. I told him a hundred times to put that bloody thing away." To my horror Vanessa's head was sticking out of the window, she'd evidently been listening this whole time. I protested, of course. The news that his mother had died in a bizarre accident is surely better coming from his father than a stranger? The man agreed, but just kept repeating the same thing: "I just don't have the courage… God help us."

He led me on a long silent walk back to his house, he would intermittently collapse in a heap of tears and I would apologise to the strangers who awkwardly circumvented around us. When we finally arrived, he gave me a set of keys. "Aren't you coming in?" I asked. "I can't... I just don't have the courage..." He said for maybe the tenth time. "OK well, where will I find Titus?" I asked, not wanting to waste time in there. "...Just follow the smell." He replied after a long beat, before turning his back on me, sitting on the curb and lighting a cigarette.

The house was plain and tidy. No sign of anything unusual except the corpse in the garden. Then it hit me. The smell. Like a reptile house filled with old people. Not coming from outside where the woman with the burnt off face lay, but upstairs. It led me to a large steel door, ominously at odds with the rest of the house. It had several locks and my trembling hands clumsily worked their way through them. I took a deep breath. This was going to be awkward.

The final key turned in the lock and after applying some force the door swung open. I was blinded by the smell. The room was empty and dark, until a pair of yellow eyes deep in a dark corner fixed themselves upon me..."Titus?" I asked tentatively. He didn't answer me vocally, but his eyes were sharp and focused. They were the same shade of yellow as the parasol. I couldn't look into them any longer so I diverted mine, instead focusing on the deep scratch marks covering the wall next to him. I cleared my throat and began. "Listen, I have some bad news to tell you I'm afraid..."

That's the last thing I remember. From the sight of my own intestines, I gather he didn't take it well. I coughed up some blood then remembered one more small detail. At the end of my explanation of how his poor mother had died, Titus asked me in a deep, terrifying voice "What is parasol?" And as I breathed my last breath, I realised that my final words on this earth were "A garden umbrella."

Judges' Profiles

Irene Baldoni

Irene is a literary agent at Georgina Capel Associates. Her list includes Fitzcarraldo Prize and Seamus Heaney First Collection Prize shortlisted authors, as well as winners of the Saltire Poetry Book Award and Fitzcarraldo Essay Prize. She previously worked at Faber & Faber and Gregory & Company Authors' Agents. Irene has an MA in Modern Literature from the University of Siena in Italy and an MA in Publishing Studies from City University, London.

Tom Robinson

Tom has been a bookseller and bookshop manager for the last twelve years. He recently left his role as manager of Foyles in Bristol to open his own independent bookshop in the city, Gloucester Road Books. He first started working in the cookery section of the Waterstones in Wimbledon Bridge, and will likely still attempt to tell you about the qualities of Lebanese cuisine if given the chance. Between 2008 and 2013, Tom co-edited *Rattle: A Journal at the Convergence of Art and Writing*. Short stories and novellas have always represented a significant portion of Tom's reading habits, and in general he would prefer reading lots of little books to fewer big ones.

Mahsuda Snaith

Mahsuda is a writer of novels and short stories. Her debut novel, *The Things We Thought We Knew*, was released in 2017 when she was named an 'Observer New Face of Fiction'. It was also selected for World Book Night in 2019. Her second novel, *How to Find Home*, was chosen as a BBC Radio 4 Book at Bedtime. In 2014 she won the SI Leeds Literary Prize and the Bristol Short Story Prize. She has led numerous creative writing workshops, is a commissioned writer for the Colonial Countryside project and her story, *The Panther's Tale*, is included in the recently published collection, *Hag: Forgotten Folktales Retold*. Mahsuda has also released a series of short, YouTube writing workshops.

Acknowledgements

Special thanks to the following people for their amazing support and contributions to this year's Bristol Short Story Prize:

Irene Baldoni, Jo Borek, Joe Burt, Jo Darque, Lu Hersey, Sandra Hopkins, Jeanette Jarvie, Richard Jones, Rosa Lovegood, Mike Manson, Bertel Martin, Catherine Mason, Louis Melia, Natasha Melia, Dave Oakley, Dawn Pomroy, Lisa Price, Thomas Rasche, Tom Robinson, Pam Smallwood and Mahsuda Snaith.

Chris Hill, Jonathan Ward, Aitana Raguán-Hernández and the 3rd year Illustration students at University of the West of England. Mimi Thebo, Billy Kahora, Amy Lehain, Andi Bullard, Gruff Kennedy and Harry Boucher at Bristol University.

Tangent Books, Foyles, Peter Morgan and Mark Furneval at ScreenBeetle, Martin Booth and Bristol 24/7.

A huge thank you, also, to all the writers who submitted their work to the 2021 Bristol Short Story Prize in what continues to be an extreme time for all. We feel very privileged to have had the opportunity to read, experience, reflect on and discuss your stories.

And finally, a massive thank you to you for buying this anthology. We hope you enjoy the collection.

2021 Bristol Short Story Prize Longlist

(Stories are listed a-z by writer)

Gayathiri Dhevi Appathurai	*Donut, Paper Napkins and Hope*
Vanwy Arif	*Migration*
Abigail Chandler	*The Retreat*
Isidora Cortes-Monroy	*Cake for the Disappeared*
Nina Cullinane	*Miss A Up the Hill*
Shona Deitch	*The Offering*
Kevin Donnellan	*The Hermit*
Louise Farr	*Rat 61*
Louise Finnigan	*Speck*
D Frankel	*Sink Rate*
Gonzalo C Garcia	*Unlikely Goals Worth Pursuing*
Susanna Gould	*A Mouthful of Nymphs*
Chris Hancock	*The Executioner*
S.P. Hannaway	*Love, Hunger*
Emily Howes	*Lane 15*
Michelle Chuqi Huang	*This Spring Never Happened*
Frances Hurd	*Jackie and Pad*
Cory Ingram	*Somewhere Up Near Ghost River*
Christopher M James	*The Villagers Who Don't Sleep*

Kate Lockwood Jefford	*Because we are Weak*
Elinor Johns	*Saturdays are Perfectly Fine*
Jessica Kashdan-Brown	*City in the Snow*
Vijay Khurana	*Follower*
Fhionna McGeechan	*Opam and Tazz*
Blaine Newton	*Life in a Bottle*
Amanda Ong	*Sifters*
Ajay Patri	*A Need for Shelter*
Hannah Persaud	*Tributaries*
Anna Polonyi	*Last Rabbit of Laysan*
Farha Tahera Quadri	*Home is the Next Place*
John Saul	*The First Time I Saw Brentford*
Annie Q. Syed	*This Is How You Lie*
Sharma Taylor	*Journal Entries of the Doubting Prophet*
Rhys Timson	*Angerland*
Sarah Tinsley	*I Don't Know What I've Lost*
Danielle Vrublevskis	*The Carnivore Club*
Amelia Walker	*The Joke Factory*
Guy Ware	*The Good Neighbour [REDACTED]*
Anna Whyat	*On Drowning*
David Winstone	*The Parasol*

Winner of the 2021 Sansom Award for Bristol writers

Stefan Mohamed   *Reservation*

Notable Contenders
(these stories were in the running for the longlist until the final decisions were made)

Fabienne Bego   *Circus Horses*
Dayne Bond   *To Be Human*
Arokoruba Cheetham-West   *That in Which We Trust*
Jane Dugdale   *The Heap*
Annie Hayter   *The Looks*
Caleb Jehl   *The Natural*
Hans Loe   *A Hymn to Your Grace*
Luke MacPherson   *State of Reunion*
Sonya Moor   *Lapin à la Moutarde*
Cassandra Passarelli   *The Great Hush*
Brian Quinn   *High Kicks and Parking Tix*
Jonathan Saint   *Message in a Bottle*
Stewart Tiley   *Heysham Notebook 5*